One

A comet could hit the earth. It could start a nuclear war by accident. Or an asteroid could boil the oceans. That's true: anything can happen. Last summer a nun in school went long distance running. And we went to London.

I suppose I should start with the row. But firstly I'm Clare Kelly and Katie's my younger sister. I'm sixteen and she's nearly fifteen. For the last three and three quarter years, we've lived with our maternal grandfather, Mr Alex Fitzgerald Esq. and his sister, Miss Brigid Fitzgerald, both of Trafalgar Road, Ranelagh, Dublin 6. This was our mother's wish. Mostly our life was ordinary. I mean, we went to school, ate meals, did homework, watched TV and sometimes played cards. But last summer everything went crazy.

It was the 15th of June. We were having breakfast in the kitchen. The dogs were snoozing in their corner - Princess, Grandfather's dog, is a ragged Scotch Terrier, while Yuppie, Aunt Brigid's, is an aristocratic King Charles Spaniel. Nothing could've been more mundane. But they looked up nervously when Grandfather came into the kitchen.

"It's another of her cracked notions! I forbid it!" he said, crossing to the dresser.

We were afraid to answer.

I rolled my eyes at Katie. She sat across the table, poking sulkily at her half-eaten porridge. A towel was wrapped around her head, and hung like a rope behind as she'd just washed her hair. School was over, so we were in dressing-gowns. Katie, who has to have everything new, wore a boy's plaid one from Clery's. Mine was an old quilted thing of Brigid's. Grandfather, of course, had eaten and already been to morning mass. As usual, he was in lumpy tweeds: grey jacket and trousers, grey jumper and socks. Even his hair was grey. The only relief was a gaily coloured silk cravat - Katie's Christmas present - which he'd lately taken to wearing as some sort of gesture to summer. It hung on his gaunt neck, reminding me of a scarecrow. And his face was frightening as he silently fussed and fumed.

Katie spooned more sugar onto her porridge. It looked disgusting. I never have anything but toast. As Brigid always said,

> *A minute in the mouth,*
> *An hour in the stomach*
> *And a lifetime on the hips*

"Sugar's poison," I muttered.

Katie shrugged maddeningly. "You believe everything you read."

There was an article in a magazine about the evils of sugar, so I gave it up. Although I now couldn't enjoy a cup of tea, I was staying off it. Your body makes its own. But I didn't remind Katie of this. I didn't want a fight. We were already in one with Grandfather.

He disappeared back to the pantry. "It's another of her cracked notions!"

On the table was a letter from our mother, stamped with the head of the Queen. It was the reason for

Grandfather's bad humour. I read the letter again. It was addressed from Heather's Knightsbridge job. And written in her familiar squiggly hand.

My darling Girls,

I want you both to come to London for the summer and enclose £50 for the fare. It's touchy here, so I've arranged chambermaiding jobs in the Cumberland Hotel. They'll put you up and feed you. Also there'll be mon for fun. In my off-time and yours, we'll have a ball. I'll expect you as soon as your exams are over - provided it's all right with your Grandfather. Wire me as soon you plan to travel and I'll meet the train. Can't wait.

Love, Heather.

We'd always called her this - which drove Grandfather crazy. He didn't approve of anything modern. Telephones, TV, videos, word processors, *et al* were the works and pomps of the Devil. According to him, mankind was slowly but surely degenerating. TV especially rotted your brain, he said, so he'd only allow us an hour a night. The irony was: he liked it better than anyone. Especially things like *Inspector Morse* and *The Equalizer*.

I poured more tea.

We were definitely going.

The clatter of dishes came from outside.

Then, over the running tap, "No good'll come of it!"

Grandfather was being idiotic. But you couldn't tell him that. You couldn't tell him anything in this humour. Or in any other.

Although Heather sent us pocket money - five pounds a week each - we hadn't seen her for nearly a year. She usually came home for the summer and we rented a house in a seaside resort like Dun Laoghaire or Bray and lived on chips and raisins. We never cooked or did anything boring. We just read books and went for walks. Or even stayed in bed. It was great. But this year there was no word of her coming.

It was killing me not to see her.

So I thought of a plan: I secretly got us chamber jobs in the London Cumberland Hotel. Then asked Heather to invite us. So her letter was only to show Grandfather. Otherwise he'd never agree. Heather's proviso about it being all right with him was only strategy too. She didn't care. They were red rags to each other. The Atlantic Ocean wouldn't be big enough to separate them, never mind the Irish Sea.

When our parents split up, Katie and I came to live with Grandfather and Brigid - she's Grandfather's younger sister. We didn't know where our father was, but Heather worked in England. She got jobs, as a companion to rich people, but she couldn't afford to have us with her. Also Grandfather had offered to send us to our mother's old school, Mount Prospect. It was mad. Cracked. But I'd agreed.

I was in a mire.

A fog.

Now I blamed myself for Heather going. I should've stopped her. I shouldn't have cared about school. It was my fault she hardly ever came home now. Sometimes, she even missed Christmas. I had bad dreams about her. Always the same dream. Katie and I were lost on the outskirts of a city. Some grey English city. Yet it couldn't be in England, because in my dream we didn't speak the language. We were looking for Heather, but could never find her.

I always awoke crying.

If only she'd come home. At the end of the summer

we'd get a flat in Dun Laoghaire - or somewhere with trees. Anywhere really. We still had school. But with part-time jobs Katie and I could help with expenses. And we'd be a family again. Just the three of us. Not Dad - he always spoiled things. "Never let a man's feet under your table," Grandfather always said. He was violently anti-him. So was Katie, who now looked miserable.

"Don't worry," I mouthed across the table. "We're going."

She sighed sulkily. "But Grandad what about?"

Mixing up word order was a crazy habit of my sister. It was some lingua franca of the third years - like "No prob!" Katie was always saying this. Also "Gluck!" for good luck. She was going into fourth year and I into fifth.

"It'll be OK," I whispered.

But there was ominous noise from the scullery.

Clatter.

Bang.

Then the back door slammed.

I put a finger to my lips.

Katie nodded, understanding we'd talk later.

In the last year my sister had really grown up. And despite a penchant for thrillers, has begun to do well at school. She has a real talent for drawing. She wants to go to the College of Art, while I'm hoping to act. Although Grandfather doesn't approve of this and says it's too like Dad. He wants me to go to the University. Or do something steady, like banking. He's a retired bank manager. But I was describing Katie. Despite all her sugar, she's tall and willowy. She has this coltish grace and looks like a Botticelli angel - pale, with long fairish hair worn in a ponytail. And grey black-lashed eyes, hidden by an unruly fringe. I'm small and plainer. My eyes are green and I've short black hair - cut in a punk style, which drives Grandfather crazy. As I said, he's antediluvian.

Like all sisters we're different. I'm casual about clothes, while Katie's particular. She's so particular, it's maddening. Like I said, she has to be in fashion and steals anything new I get. Clothes are one of the things we fight over.

Just then Brigid came into the kitchen. Seeing Katie's face, her own crumpled and she said in her husky voice. "Don't fret, pet."

Katie stabbed her porridge. "It's fair not!"

"Talk properly," I said. Sometimes I'm too impatient with her.

But Brigid grimaced in sympathy. As long as I could remember, our aunt had always looked the same. She's one of these people who stick at the age of thirty - probably she was born thirty. She's a neat small person, and youngish, compared to Grandfather. With dyed blonde hair gathered into a velvet bow at the nape of her neck. Also, she wears fashionable clothes, although never denim. And make-up, especially rouge. She has this thing about youth and says calling her "Aunt" makes her feel geriatric. She is, really. She's our grandaunt, for God's sake, but you can't say it. You can't even think it. She'd just been smoking. I knew. I was expert at detecting symptoms - pepperminty breath and a guilty look. She always has cigarettes hidden somewhere in the house, constantly moving them to be one step ahead of Grandfather, who abhors them. If you use the bathroom after Brigid, you can smell them. I don't know how she can risk her health. She gives them to Katie too. I know. While Grandfather'd been giving out ructions, our Aunt had fled upstairs for a fag. Not that she wouldn't take our side. She would. It was just typical of her to say nothing. She couldn't stand rows and believed discretion to be the better part, sort of. Besides, she was terrified of Grandfather.

Everyone was, except Katie.

She kept up the game with her food. And her words. "Grandad's in a moody bad."

Then Grandfather came back, freezing everyone with a glare.

Brigid composed her face, passing me *The Irish Times*.

Grandfather's eyes glinted bluely. "I heard that, Miss!"

Katie pushed away her plate. She's the type who shows all her emotions by going beetroot. She did this now.

Grandfather's mouth tightened. "When you've finished wasting good food, you can do that weeding!"

Katie hated weeding - we both did. But she got up langourously and, carrying her plate to the scullery, washed it with exaggerated obedience.

"And take that towel off your head. Do you think you're the Ayatollah?"

"My hair's wet!"

"Well, dry it! Don't come to the table like that!"

"You made me!"

It was true. Grandfather had called her from the bathroom, insisting that the porridge would get cold. He couldn't deny that. Anyhow he hated home truths. So no one ever argued with him, except Katie. She quite often cheeked him. Compared to me, she got away with murder. As the eldest, I always got it.

As Katie passed back through the kitchen to the hall, her hands were thrust deep in her dressing-gown pockets and her bath towel swayed defiantly.

I was waiting for an explosion, but Grandfather

Has Anyone Seen Heather?

turned on the dogs instead. "Out, you two! Out!"

Princess scampered obediently to the door, but Yuppie, of course, acted up - it's true about animals taking on the characteristics of their owners. Yuppie's a real *prima donna*. As Grandfather whooshed her out, Brigid picked her up, hugging her possessively.

"Is the gate closed?" she asked.

"Of course it is!" Grandfather snapped.

Brigid petted Yuppie's pert head, pulling her long floppy ears. "We don't want to go outside, do we?"

Grandfather sighed resignedly. "I thought you were folding the towels?"

"Sorry, I forgot!" Brigid's always saying sorry. She's one of those very nervous people and sometimes disappears into a mental home. Sometimes she imagines people are breaking into the house. She leaves bits of string around to catch them. She has this weird obsession that Grandfather prevented her from getting married. It's embarrassing. She falls in love with all sorts of people. Sometimes the gardener or the postmen, whom she thinks are famous people in disguise. She throws them notes out the window when she's bad. Or scented hankies, which she keeps in her drawer. She used to write to James Mason. And once she fell in love with a government minister, and thought he was giving her a message every time he was on TV. She even thought the priest was secretly signalling from the altar every time he blew his nose.

"Well, don't just stand there!" Grandfather shouted at her now. I have to admit, he wasn't the most patient person.

"I'm going!" Clutching Yuppie, Brigid followed Katie out.

There were no orders for me.

I hid behind *The Irish Times* - our English teacher,

Sister Martin, had told me to read it during the holidays. She's the only nice nun in school, all the others are drips. I've always liked her brown eyes. She was hoping I'd get an A in English in the Leaving. Thanks to my Dad, I'd seen a lot of Shakespeare. According to him, the Bard told us more about ourselves than any other dramatist - although we knew less about him than any other writer. Dad was always saying this. Then why couldn't he learn from Othello, the batterer? Look what had happened to Desdemona. I mean, was it really necessary? I asked him this once, but that's another story. It's in the past and there's nothing more boring. I preferred thinking about the future. Things like acting in *Hamlet*. I wanted to be in it. "How now, Lord Hamlet?" was so much more interesting than "Hello." And "To be or not to be" summed everything up. I knew it by heart. But lately I hadn't worked at school. I'd got dreamy. And now I couldn't concentrate on the paper. I was expecting an explosion with Grandfather. Although I hadn't Katie's nerve, I'd learnt one thing: you got nowhere by weakness. So I pretended to read.

At first he just pottered round the kitchen.

If I said anything, he'd only pick on me. So I stared at the blurred print.

He rooted noisily in the cupboard.

Soon there was an irritated humming.

I ignored it.

"Clare, where's the lemon squeezer?"

I pretended not to hear.

"Clare!"

I looked up vaguely. "Wh-what?"

"Stop acting!"

"I'm not!"

"You heard me!"

I felt myself redden. Grandfather could see right through me. He always could. "Why do you want it?"

"For the rhubarb jam. If I don't make it today, the rhubarb will go off!" His glare was of the, 'I have to do everything myself' variety. It was peculiar, a man making jam. But as Brigid hated cooking, he did most of it. It was a job, getting Brigid to do anything.

I went to look. "It should be there."

There was all sorts of clutter in the big pine dresser - plates of every description on the top shelves, and smaller things on the bottom ones. But no sign of the lemon squeezer.

As I stood up, a jam dish fell out, smashing on the red quarry tiles. "Gosh, sorry!"

Grandfather glared. He'd come to the boil.

"I - I'll buy you another."

He picked it up. "It's irreplaceable!"

I got the dustpan and brush from the scullery. "That's ridiculous."

"How dare you! It's your Aunt Brigid's - and hand painted!"

It was a mistake to argue with him, but I did. "It's only a jam dish."

"You've no respect for property! That's the trouble with today's young!"

I thought the Russians were right, basically, but I was sorry about the dish. I really was. Still I said, "Property is theft."

There was flint in Grandfather's blue eyes. "I'm sick of your socialist nonsense!"

"I don't believe in private property, Grandfather."

"So you break your aunt's dishes!"

"It was an accident!"

"That convent has been corrupted by Marxist friars!"

This was the priest who taught us Religous

Education. Grandfather disapproved because he was for Nicaragua and talked about liberation theology. Also he didn't wear black. But it was mean to pick on the priest now, just because I'd upset him. But I couldn't deny my beliefs.

I sighed heavily. "It's nothing to do with socialism."

"He's corrupted you and now you're corrupting the child!"

The "child" was my sister. She was quite young when we came to live with Grandfather, so the two old people were especially fond of her. Fussing over her health, etc. Now that the holidays had come, we were leaving. In a way it was unfair to them. But we had Heather.

I put the broken bits into the outside bin.

When I came back, Grandfather was still in the kitchen.

I passed to the door, muttering. "Katie thinks for herself."

He just stared after me. "Where are you going now?"

"Into town. Then I have work." I had a summer job in a cinema to help with pocket money and clothes.

"I was hoping for help with the jam." His voice was gentler.

"I can't. Katie's here."

Grandfather brushed at a wisp of hair. He did this when weakening. "I'm sorry I got cross. It doesn't matter about the dish. Can't you stay home this morning?"

"I have to see someone - about a book."

He perused my face. "You're meeting that young man!"

"No," I lied, looking at the ground. "I have to return a book."

Grandfather's mouth tightened. I was at the door

when he suddenly pleaded. "Wait, Clare please!"

I obeyed.

Grandfather wore his years well. He always said worrying about us kept him young. But standing in the doorway, he looked old and frail. "I hope you're not taking your mother's hare-brained scheme seriously."

I stared at the willow-patterned plates on the wall over the dresser, avoiding eye-contact. His look was worse than anything. It told me how much he'd miss us, despite always giving out.

"You're a sensible girl, Clare."

"We have to go, Grandfather, it's ..."

"But you have a job here."

There was no way I could explain about Heather. "I'll tell them this afternoon."

He reddened in anger. "Well, that's a nice thing ... walking out!"

"I'm not walking out!"

He sighed. "What do you call it, then?"

"But London'll be fun," I pleaded. "And we can earn money."

"Money, I'm all for. But your mother's idea of fun isn't mine. As you well know!"

It was always, "your mother." Never, "my daughter." Or even "Heather." Would their quarrel never end?

"Well, I forbid you to bring the child!"

"But Heather -."

"You know my opinion of your mother!" His old anger at Heather had flared up. How long did you have to suffer for a mistake? Heather'd never be forgiven for getting pregnant and running away with our father. He was an American, an unemployed actor who'd turned out to be a drunk. And gave her a nervous breakdown. Several nervous breakdowns. She took pills and stayed in bed and gave up eating. When she was bad, I didn't know what to do.

Turning, Grandfather stamped out to the scullery.

I fled upstairs.

I hated upsetting Grandfather. I loved him really - he and Brigid were the only relations we had. He couldn't be better to Katie and me. After all, he'd taken us both in. He paid our school fees and regularly bought us clothes. And cooked meals and worried about us. It was unfair that a mother had more rights. But there was no commandment to honour a grandfather. Heather had only to agree and we were off.

Upstairs Brigid was putting towels away in the landing cupboard. Yuppie played with a slipper at her feet. Seeing me, she came running over and clutched my hand. "Clare, take me with you!"

I reddened. "I can't."

Brigid has this way of handling you. It irritated me, but I never said anything. She couldn't take it. She couldn't take much. Her hair was slightly askew now, and she'd obviously worked herself into a state. She was a dreamer like Heather. Running away was another of her obsessions. She believed you could start life again at seventy. Her happiness had been ruined, she believed, by Grandfather, of all people. But she'd find it again in some foreign country - America or Africa. It was mental. Grandfather had inherited her. He'd always looked after her. Sometimes, she'd pick a row with him and pack her case and run away. But some stranger would always bring her home. Or else, she'd phone from the airport or station. Then Grandfather would send me in a taxi to collect her. Afterwards they wouldn't talk to each other, so Katie and I would have to be go-betweens. "Ask your grandfather to pass the salt ... Please tell your Aunt Brigid ..."

She rubbed my hands worriedly. "London's a dangerous place! You're too young to go alone."

"It's full of Irish. And Heather'll be there." What would we do with a geriatric aunt?

Brigid smiled slowly. "Poor Heather ... poor, dear child. I'd love to see her again."

"We'll bring her home." I decided not to tell her about the flat. She'd only tell Grandfather and I wanted to wait for the right moment. You had to pick your moment with Grandfather.

She clutched my hand tighter. "Please, take me with you!"

I shook my head. "There's nowhere for you to stay."

"But you're so young."

"I'm sixteen and a half."

"But I wasn't allowed out alone at that age."

Gently, I released my hand. Stooping I reached to pet Yuppie. "It's different now, Brigid."

"But Katie's only a baby."

"She's fifteen."

"She's fourteen."

"She'll be fifteen in a month."

I groaned. Dammit, we were teenagers. "I can take care of her."

Brigid went back to her towels, muttering, "Poor little Katie."

It got me the way she and Grandfather thought we were such kids. I wanted to shout, it's not Victorian times now. A few of my class aren't even virgins. Including me. Almost. But I didn't. Anyhow you can't argue with some people. That's true, 'Enry 'Iggins. So I went upstairs to dress. Then headed into town to meet Wally.

Two

In Westmoreland Street, I bought tickets. Then wired Heather:

*SAILING TOMORROW NIGHT. SEE YOU SOON.
LOVE CLARE.*

Then I went to meet Wally in Bewley's. He's my boyfriend. The girls in school are dead impressed because he's doing Arts in college. But we're only platonic. I'm not like Brigid - romance isn't for me. It's a cracked way to organize the world. If I ever marry, it won't be for love. It'll be someone with brains - like Wally, only better looking. And maybe a deeper voice.

It was summer, so Bewley's fire wasn't lit. Wally and I always met in the same booth. It was free that day so I settled into its plush red velvet to wait. I loved the smell of coffee, the old fashioned atmosphere and clink of cups. Imagine, Bewley's was there when Grandfather was young. And Heather always says it's the one place in Dublin that hasn't changed. But lately they'd been taken over. It was self-service now. And the buns were different. And they sold sandwiches in tacky plastic packets. Still, there were nice plants and a mock cherry tree in one room.

Luckily I had two hours before work.

I took out a book on Sartre - Wally'd lent it to me.

Philosophy was my latest thing.

Especially existentialism.

I cringed at my utter fascist past. School was so conservative, it killed me. It was absolutely antediluvian about women. They still had customs from when Heather was young - like weekly Cards for good behaviour. In Heather's day, they were called Notes. But it's the same idiotic system. They treat us like kids and don't care at all about politics. Worst of all, they get personal. Why can't you just go to school, do your work and go home at four o'clock? Why did they pry as well? Somehow, Sister Martin had heard about Wally. And our parents splitting up. And she was always on at me about mass. I was afraid to tell her I'd lost my faith. But so had Sartre. According to him, existence is prior to essence and one has to be socially committed. Above all, the individual is free. I didn't understand about essence, etc. But I knew it was too protected with Grandfather. Life was awaiting me. At my age Africans had children. But I was still stuck in the rut of childhood. Sixteen was pushing it. I mean, both of us were old enough to be married, never mind go away for the summer. Although foreign countries scared me, London would be OK. I was there once with Heather. And this time I'd have Katie.

At least we could speak the language.

My mind kept wandering onto what the future held. My stomach churned with nerves. For the first time I was taking action. But I was dreading telling them at work. The pay was good for a schoolgirl. And they'd made a great compliment about taking me - you were meant to be eighteen. But I had a forged ID. It was a cinch, you got a form from USIT, then filled in your age with a rub-out biro. Then got your headmistress to sign it. Then changed your age later. I had one for Katie too. According to them, she was seventeen and I eighteen.

"Hello, Clare," a squeaky voice said at my elbow.

It was Wally.

"Hi."

Has Anyone Seen Heather?

He plonked down opposite, taking off his wire intellectual glasses to clean them. Despite the summer, he was still lost in his big college Arts scarf. He has brilliant blue eyes, a pert nose, and a small pony tail. Everything about him's small. But he's wiry. Maybe his glasses make him seem older. Or maybe his seriousness about everything. But he's not macho and is for women's rights. Also he's brilliant. And writes poetry. He's even published some. Over the last year we'd spent hours measuring out our lives with coffee spoons. There was nothing we couldn't talk about.

I shut my book.

"Sorry, I'm late." He put on his glasses.

"That's OK." He'd come on the bus from Belfield.

"How are you getting on with Sartre?"

I shrugged. Truthfully, I wasn't. "Well, you know ..."

"*L'Etre et le Néant's* probably his most socially significant work." Wally pronounced French properly.

I couldn't admit my difficulties with existence and essence.

"Of course, you know it's derivative from Heidegger's *Sein und Zeit*?"

"No - I didn't."

Wally cleared his throat. He always did this before lecturing me. "You don't have to worry about that. Most people think of Sartre as a philosopher - which is an injustice. His novels are much more relevant. Did you finish *La Nausée*?"

I nodded again. I'd loathed it, but couldn't admit it.

Luckily he stood up and didn't quiz me further. He took a sheet of typed paper from his pocket. "Read this, while I get coffee."

It was a poem:

the shell
the waves washed up a coral shell
and I knew I'd heard before what
this shell would have me hear:
that it was a common thing,
every human has at will:
to love, to hate, to give, to take.
nothing costly, not an ecstasy.
so back to sea I threw my shell.
the sea, so full of pain
tumultuous grief and peace
would not listen to an empty shell
with a mocking tale to tell.

"What do you think?" he came back with the tray.

Although I only like poetry that rhymes, I said, "It's good. But there's no capital letters."

"That's my style. Have you never read e e cummings?"

"No."

"Well, he doesn't use them either. The important thing is, do you understand it?"

"Of course!" God, I wasn't that thick. "Don't you think you need a line in the middle. I mean, you pick up the shell. Shouldn't you put it to your ear?"

He slurped his coffee. "No, that's understood. You see, it's about the great passions. I don't want to be bourgeois, Clare."

"Well, you're not," I said nervously. I hoped he wasn't talking about us. I couldn't feel great passion for him.

"You see, the bourgeoisie don't really live."

I nodded.

"They just exist ..." he went on lecturing in that vein. Asking him something was like pushing a button.

Conversation cascaded from him. He told me all sorts of things. Like a table's not really a table. It's just our projection of reality. A collection of atoms. He was always telling me to "think cosmically." That mankind is nothing and our life is the dance of a butterfly. About the Ozone layer. And global warming. And stars, and Halley's Comet visiting the earth every seventy-six years. It came last in 1986. Now they think it's from deep space and not the Oort Cloud - that's at the edge of our solar system. Comets are snowballs a mile wide. One hit the earth in Russia and turned into diamonds. Halley's is coming back in 2062. Imagine, I'll be eighty-nine. I'll definitely see it then. It goes the opposite way to everything else in the universe - just like Katie and me, living with Grandfather and not our parents.

Wally's brain made up for any lack in his appearance. Ours was a case of unreciprocated love, just like the Queen in *A Midsummer Night's Dream* - my Dad once had a part in that. Although I couldn't return his feelings, Wally didn't mind. As I said, everyone in school was dead jealous. He'd brought me to the Concert Hall to hear Verdi's *Requiem*. And on a march to the Dáil in support of divorce. He's for abortion, which Sister Martin says is murder. We planned to meet over the summer in London as he was working there too.

He laughed when I told him about the row with Grandfather. "You won't have to clock-in in London."

This was a dig that I had to be home by eleven - which makes it awkward for plays, etc. Grandfather always waited up for me. He sat darning socks in the kitchen - it was a foible of his to darn our socks. Everyone else in the world threw them out, but he couldn't stand waste. Or else he played Solitaire by himself in the drawing room. He always quizzed me about what we'd seen and sort of perused my face. Oh, he was lenient enough with us, compared to the stories Brigid told us about Heather's youth. But I knew he didn't like the idea of Wally being older. Also he was afraid of me drinking, although he needn't have been. I'd taken the pledge. I'd made a sort of bargain with God that if I didn't drink, ever, my Dad might give it up. It was cracked, considering there was most probably no one out there. At least, that's what Wally says.

"I suppose he worries," I sipped my coffee.

"You're old enough to look after yourself."

I squirmed inwardly. I hated being treated so "young." "Well, you know, Katie's ..."

"She's old enough too. The nuclear family keeps youth in a false position of dependency."

"I suppose so." I didn't remind him Grandfather wasn't exactly nuclear. And we were hardly a family.

"He shouldn't push you around," he went on pompously.

He didn't like Grandfather and called him an imperialist.

"Has he got legal custody?"

"No."

I fiddled anxiously with my spoon. I was over the age, but Katie could still be sent to a home. Social workers had called to see Grandfather once. But I didn't want to talk about them. The very thought of them gave me the the creeps. So I changed the subject. "Let's buy a sandwich and eat it in the Green."

He nodded. "OK."

It's not quite true that I tell Wally everything. I've never told him the whole story of our Dad. I've never told anyone, not even Sister Martin, that he hit us. Or how Grandfather had stuck up for us. Actually he didn't have legal custody. I suppose our parents still did. Or at least our parent - we didn't count our father. And it was too difficult to explain that Grandfather just doted on Katie. And his thinking us children was too embarrassing.

In the end we had a salad in O'Sullivan's on the corner of Dawson Street. Wally paid, which I wasn't happy with. I was sixteen now and old enough to cope. But I gave in when he insisted, saying he wouldn't be seeing me for weeks. O'Sullivan's is like a French café and you can sit outside and watch the world go by. A girl from school passed and I waved. It was awful, but I loved being seen with Wally.

Afterwards he walked me down to my cinema in Abbey Street - I can't say which because of my faked ID. He walked funnily, sort of on the balls of his feet, with his chin jutting forwards and talking non-stop. As always I listened, nodding at all the right places. And we parted with a kiss, promising to meet in London. In the foyer the other two usherettes were lined up in their grey and red uniforms with torches in hand. Miss Murray, the chief usherette, was inspecting them. She'd been there since the year dot and still did things the old way. She looked like an ancient silent movie actress. She had black-dyed, tightly permed hair, wizened rouge-blotched cheeks and a scarlet cupid mouth.

"You're late, Clare," she snapped.

I waited while she gave the day's pep talk - it was about taking too long for our tea break. It was horrible. Despite the modernisation - I mean the two cinemas and that - we had to get water from a sink in a lavatory. It was full of horrible brown-stained cups and used tea bags, which reminded me of dead mice. I shivered going in there.

When she dismissed us, I told her about London.
Her mouth tightened. "But you're giving no notice."
"I didn't know."
"You won't get your wages if you walk out."
"But -."
"Hurry to your post now."
I stood my ground. "Could I see the manager?"
"He isn't available."

God, it was unfair. I mean, they owed me nearly a week's pay. If I walked out, I'd never get it. And, as Heather was by no means rich, we'd need the money in London. I should've stood my ground. But I went to change.

The ads had started by the time I was at my post in Cinema 2. As usual, it took my eyes a minute to adjust to the dark. Since it was a summer afternoon, there were only a few people sprinkled through the rows. Phil, the other usherette I was friends with, had seen them to their seats. So there was nothing else to do, except flash a torch if people came in late. I thought I'd learn about acting from the job, but was always bored into a trance. Unlike plays, once is enough for most movies. That day I could only think of my money.

I really needed it.

During the interval Frank Sinatra started crooning over the loud speaker, *Smoke Gets in Your Eyes*.

It was Heather's song. And although they played it every day, it always brought a lump to my chest. Suddenly her voice was singing in my head. She was a real romantic. Because of her I was antediluvian about music. I liked only old songs, while Katie was into things like Enya and Sinead O'Connor - she has posters of her on the wall. Also Bono and The Edge. Lately she follows a group called The Cure. Their fans are weirdos called Cureheads with disgusting red lips and spiky hair. You see them drinking cider in the park. My great fear was Katie becoming one. I mean, she wanted a pair of skinhead boots - Doc Marten's, for God's sake.

Heather's voice was now blotting out the singer's. *"They asked me how I knew ... my true love was true ..."*

Heather was daft. I could see her now, dancing round our old kitchen with a cup of tea in her hand. We were renting a flat in Drumcondra. I'd been invited to a boy's twelfth birthday party. Daddy had rehearsal and said it was too far anyhow. I was fed up, but she winked, whispering, "Leave it to me."

"But I've nothing to wear."

She hummed on.

There was no money. But somehow she got me a blue corduroy dress in a little shop in Dorset Street. It had a white lace collar. She washed my hair and asked for the keys of the car. She was going to drive me, even though she was only learning and couldn't reverse properly.

In the end Daddy gave in.

It was abnormal to care so much for a mother. Most girls in school fought with theirs. They had snaps of their boyfriends while I had one of Heather. They wanted to go au-pairing. Or picking grapes in France. Or round Europe by train. I know I should've been living my own life. But I couldn't. I just longed for ... oh,

The touch of a vanished hand
And the sound of a voice that was still.

It was death without her. Besides, she needed me to mind her.

Then Phil came over, whispering, "See your man in the second row?"

I peered through the dark. "What about him?"

Her blackened eyes rounded. "Oh, my sheriff."

I thought she must have OD'd on cowboys in childhood. She lived for "filums" and was always seeing movie stars in the Savoy. Last week Paul Newman was in. And the week before Peter O'Toole. It didn't occur to her that people of their wealth had VCR's. Probably their own cinemas. They wouldn't be coming to Dublin. But it was no use pointing this out. I just said reasonably, "A sheriff'd be wearing a big hat."

She blinked. "What?"

"Sheriffs wear big hats. And stars."

"Sheriffs? No, it's Omar Sharif!"

"Oh!" I peered at the man again.

"Isn't he fab?"

I nodded patiently. "Maybe he'll give you an autograph on the way out."

Phil skipped back to her place for the short film about canoeing. She was daft, but I liked her. The line between madness and normality is faint. It really is.

There was a lot of white water in the short film. I imagined hurtling down that river. Away from our stuffy darkness and the reek of cigarettes and popcorn. I'd seen the main film too often to laugh at the jokes. It was *Desperately Seeking Susan* with Madonna. I liked her, but old movies were better. Ones with Greta Garbo and Cary Grant. Or Tyrone Power in *Marie Antoinette*. Or Laurence Olivier in *Emma, Lady Hamilton*. I'm really antidiluvian. But Madonna's clothes were OK. I liked looking at them.

That day I couldn't stop thinking of my money. Why couldn't they pay me?

I decided on a strategy - I'd scream like a maniac. Then they'd be sorry. I tried to muster up the courage. Several times I opened my mouth but nothing happened. Then about half- an-hour into the film, I let out a shriek.

Phil hurried over. "What is it?"

I did it again.

By now the patrons were turning round. And the doorman was running down the aisle to me.

Phil was shaking me. "Stop it, Clare!"

I ignored her.

Seeing it was me, the doorman whispered, "What's up, love?"

I kept on.

He looked worried. "What's wrong, me oul flower?"

Several people ran in my direction.

The doorman grabbed my arm and pulled me gently but firmly to the door. "Quiet, now!"

Outside in the foyer, he looked at me worriedly. "I'll ring for Miss Byrne."

After a few minutes she came puffing up the stairs. "What was all that noise?"

He told her.

"What happened, Clare?"

"It just comes on me."

Her eyes rounded. "What?"

"Sort of claustrophobia." I'd read about that causing a panic attack.

She perused my face. "You're very pale."

"I'll be all right."

But she brought me into the Ladies and sat guarding me, while the doorman went for a cup of tea. While I sipped it, she watched me, swallowing slowly, as if getting up the courage to say something.

"You'll be all right, dear," she said, finally.

I nodded. "I can go back in now."

She cleared her throat. "Ah - but you wanted to see the manager?"

"Oh, no. I'll give proper notice."

But she stood up and, clutching my arm, brought me to the manager's office. It had worked. He waived the rule about notice and paid me for a week extra.

Three

Grandfather's right: I'm always acting. And there's enough madness in the world without adding to it. I know this from personal experience, ie, my Dad. And Brigid. So I didn't tell Katie about the Savoy. It'd be bad example. Also she might tell Brigid, who'd tell Grandfather, who'd have a fit.

Grandfather gnawed at my heart.

If only he'd agree.

I waited till after dinner to bring up the subject again. Grandfather usually played cards with Brigid then - at least, he did when they weren't quarrelling. He really enjoyed this, so it was his best time of day. Yuppie and Princess always lay in front of the hearth. That evening, as we'd no homework, we joined in.

Grandfather looked over his glasses at the kitty - a copper saucer with some coins. It made his day to win a few pence at Rummy. And he was doing well that evening, much to Brigid's irritation.

After a few games, I said, "I got the sailing tickets, Grandfather."

There was a deadly silence.

Brigid finished dealing.

Grandfather picked up his cards, clutching them as if he'd never let them go.

The atmosphere thickened.

Brigid studied her hand, hissing tensely through her teeth.

"We're off tomorrow, Grandfather." I tried again.

"We're boating the take!" my sister joked stupidly.

"Play, Katie!" was all Grandfather said, his knuckles white. He was definitely ignoring me.

Sneaking a look at my sister, I sorted out my sequences.

She threw down a card, chatting nervously. "We'll see Buckingham Palace, and the museums. And the Tower of London. And Scotland Yard ..."

"If you don't end up there!"

"But why should we?" I asked.

"Yes, why?" Katie looked up from her hand.

There was another deadly silence.

Brigid caught my eye, then rolled her eyes warningly at the ceiling.

Grandfather deftly re-organized his cards. "You're obviously determined on this folly, Clare. So go! And good riddance! But don't think you can come back!"

Brigid tut-tutted under her breath.

It was total war. Grandfather meant it. He'd treated Heather the same way. Thrown her out forever because he didn't approve of her husband. Well, it wouldn't be like that between Heather and us. Most definitely not.

My hand trembled. "We *have* to go, Grandfather."

"You mean you *want* to!"

I didn't answer.

"At least, be honest!"

"You don't understand ..."

"I've nothing more to say, Clare."

"But -."

"The subject is closed!"

I said nothing more either.

It was awful. Why was he acting like this? We finished our game in miserable silence and went up to bed.

Katie and I shared a cheerful bedroom with her posters on the wall. Usually she plugged in headphones and listened to music before going to sleep, while I always read. But that night she wanted to chat. "What'll we do in London?" she asked. Or, "Would Heather come home with us?" She kept it up for so long that I couldn't sleep at all. Crazily I kept thinking of that blue corduroy dress when I was twelve. Heather always went to such trouble for us. I think we got closer because of my Dad. He couldn't get any acting work, so he drank. And that made him violent. It was a vicious circle. They had screaming rows. Once I was at the top of the stairs, listening. Heather was in her night-gown, crying. "I'm not giving you the car keys!"

Our father was handsome - I mean, picture someone like William Hurt, only unsuccessful. He had the same blue eyes, the same burly shape and thinning hair. But now he was completely red in the face and lunged at Heather drunkenly. She jumped out of the way. So he grabbed a dish from the dresser and smashed it. "Give them to me!"

"No!"

He smashed another. "Give them to me!"

"No!"

He smashed another. "All right, you bitch! Here goes the family china!"

Then another.

And another.

I started crying. It wasn't fair, calling her names.

Then Heather saw me on the stairs. "Go back to bed," she whispered.

I did - like a coward. He beat her up and locked her out. For hours. With nothing on. But I didn't know. I didn't know.

Of course, he got the keys and woke up in jail.

It was dawn before I heard Heather crying in the garden. Why'd I gone to sleep? How could I? What kind of daughter was I? Heather depended on me. Who was minding her now?

I lay there imagining the flat we'd have. It'd be small but cosy, with a bedroom between us girls, and one for Heather. She'd have to have her own room with a large wardrobe for all her clothes. And she'd like a garden - although Katie'd be irritated by having to weed. I'd miss Grandfather and Brigid, but they'd visit. And bring Yuppie and Princess. Everything'd be OK. We'd make money in London. And Grandfather'd give us sheets and things. I kept imagining for hours, but when I finally slept I had my dream. It was always the same. Katie and I were lost. This time we were waiting for a bus in the city centre. We waited and waited in some bleak ghetto. All cement pavements, without a tree in sight. A bus came at last, but the conductor pushed us off. Then, somehow, we were on an Underground train. We went round and round, getting nowhere. I woke up so sad.

Why couldn't Grandfather agree? Of course, he was right: we did want to go. I'd plotted the whole thing, but couldn't admit it. Grandfather never lied or evaded anything. He was an upright person. He'd have been furious if he'd known about the cinema. But he didn't suffer from nerves. And he'd never understand about Heather.

I was jaded the next day and went through the

motions of packing like a zombie. Grandfather kept his word. He said nothing more about us going. He said nothing all the next day. He just told Brigid to give us an early dinner, so we wouldn't miss the boat. And when we were going, he wouldn't even say goodbye.

We patted the dogs in the kitchen. Princess was calm as usual, but Yuppie knew something was up. I think she knew we were going. Then Brigid kissed us. There were tears on her papery cheeks and her breath reeked of cigarettes.

I pointed to my mouth and mimed someone smoking. "Remember, don't smoke too much."

She pulled herself up to her full height. "I don't know what you mean!"

"I mean don't risk your health."

Brigid screwed up her eyes suspiciously. "Have you been spying on me?"

"Of course not!"

Then Katie hugged her tightly. "Gluck, Brigid."

Brigid pulled away, looking injured. "Take me with you!"

I soothed her. "We can't!"

She humphed, then reaching into her cardigan pocket took out four new English tenners. "Well, this is for emergencies."

I pushed her hand away. "You can't afford it."

But she put the money in each of our pockets. "Take it! I'll worry less."

I hesitated. "Well, we'll pay you back."

Katie hugged her again. "Look after Grandad."

I picked up our case. "Say goodbye for us."

And next thing we were heading for the gate and down Trafalgar Road.

We took the bus to town and then the Dart to Dun Laoghaire. Crowds had already gathered at the mailboat. And the usual line of emigrants laden down with luggage waited to be let on. We joined them, dragging our cases up the ramp and onto the creaky boat. On the first deck, the men already waited for the bar to open, while the women called nervously to their children. We kept seats in the downstairs lounge and then went back on deck.

Katie ran excitedly to the railings. "Hope I'm not sick."

"It won't be rough," I said.

But I was wrong.

I often wonder what'd it be like to foretell the future. Would it affect your actions? As we watched from the deck that summer night, we couldn't guess what lay ahead. How we'd be thrown on life's surge and have to cross metaphorical mountains. We were just two normal girls excited to be seeing our mother soon. We were mad with excitement. It's crazy, but it seemed like we were conquering the world.

At last there was a hooting noise and the ship's engine revved up, pulling us out into the cold grey water. We waved at the people left on the wharf and then at those standing on the pier's arm. Behind us the sun disappeared into the Dublin hills. With Dalkey, Howth and the island of Ireland's Eye, they were like humps of sleeping whales. Or monsters waiting for a summons. The salt wind stung our faces, but we kept on waving till we were far out to sea, and the people on shore had disappeared into the black line of the land.

Four

At Euston there was no sign of Heather.

Katie looked sleepily round the platform. "Did you send the wire?"

I scanned it to the end. "Of course. It was a night letter. She got it yesterday morning."

At the mid hour of night we'd changed to a train. Then we were hurtled endlessly through Wales in the dark and disgorged, bleary-eyed, there in the grey dawn. I don't really have a sense of place, especially of London. Although we were to spend that summer there, we went nearly everywhere by Underground. It was just huge. I remember the pizzas. And Marks and Spencers. And parks with iron railings and other railings stopping you crossing the road. And red buses screeching up and down streets. And traffic churning ceaselessly, clanking and spluttering like some sort of mechanical dragon. But all that was in the future. For now we had to cope with Euston. Its platform was typical: vast and noisy and smelling of grime and burnt rubber.

Grabbing her case, Katie started up it. "She must be here."

The other passengers had dispersed by now. Either they'd been met, or had headed off to taxis or the Underground. We dragged our cases past the British Rail barricade and looked round again.

The main station was newer and brighter than the platform, with all sorts of snack and hamburger places. Although it was still early, bowler-hatted men already rushed to escalators and main-line platforms.

"The six forty-five train to Cardiff will leave from platform seven," a muffled voice came over the loudspeaker.

There was still no Heather. We looked at each other.

"It's ironic," my sister said.

"Whatever it is, it's not irony!"

"There's no need to be bitchy."

I glared at my sister. It was typical of her to use words she didn't understand. But I'd been mean, so said more gently, "Then stop talking through your hat."

What could've happened?

I left Katie minding the cases and checked the café. People sat at the tables eating, while others queued for food. But Heather wasn't among them.

Then I tried the huge Super Loo, scanning the women at the washbasins and lingering hopefully by closed cubicle doors.

But no luck.

I went to the main entrance. Outside the traffic pounded anonymously. On the way back I saw a computer portrait on a notice board of a man with a beard.

HAVE YOU SEEN THIS MAN?
On the 20th of May, a man answering this description attacked a woman in a first-class carriage of the Cardiff train. If you have seen him, please contact the police at any station.

The place was sinister. Oh God, what were we to do? Where was Heather? This wasn't like her. When we were young she was obsessively punctual and always got mad if we were late. Something had happened.

Controlling my panic, I went back to Katie.

She sat on a rucksack, her chin resting on her fists. Her long blonde hair fell to her shoulders, contrasting with her red anorak. She had her headphones in. She always has them in. Music's like a soother to her.

"Maybe you sent the wire to the wrong address," she said, pulling them out.

I sighed tiredly. "I didn't."

Just then a tramp ambled up, his grubby hand out. "God bless you, love."

There was a dead look in his eyes. He smelled of drink, so I stiffened. But Katie dug into her pocket and gave him fifty pence.

His eyes lit up and he touched his forehead. "I'll pray for you."

I groaned at my sister. "We couldn't afford 50p."

"Don't be stingy."

"Someone has to be responsible."

My sister arched her eyebrows under her fringe.

Maybe it was tiredness, or the bleakness of the station, but I could've killed her. True, I was sometimes too careful, but she's irresponsible about money. On the boat over she kept going for tea. She was like someone on a drip.

"You sent it to the wrong address," she persisted now.

"I didn't."

"Are you sure?"

"Yes."

I checked my address book again. I'd sent the night letter to 26A Walton Street. It was the right address. What if Heather had mixed up the days? Or we kept missing her? We might run out of money before our first payday. I checked my shoulder bag for my wallet - it was still there. And Brigid's twenty pounds was inside. But how far would that go in London?

I nudged my sister. "Is your money safe?"

"It's in my rucksack."

"Make sure."

She unzipped her rucksack, groping for her purse. "Here it is."

"How much have you left?"

"Seventeen pounds."

"Put it in your jeans pocket."

"It's OK there."

"Do as you're told."

She pulled a face. "OK."

I ignored her, sitting down too. Luckily we were comfortably dressed in jeans and trainers. As the elder, I was in charge. There was nothing to be gained by quarrelling. And it was useless to panic. Or move from the bench. Heather would turn up. She was a little late, that's all. So we settled down to wait, taking turns to go for tea - we didn't want to waste money on food. The station gradually filled up and life rushed past in its own inexorable way. But for us the time dragged awfully, our hopes dying with each endless minute.

Finally I phoned Heather's work number.

Someone in the next phone was shouting, so I could hardly hear. But then a woman's voice answered, "Hello."

It sounded Northern English or Scottish.

"Could I speak to Mrs Kelly?"

There was a sharp intake of breath. Then the voice snapped, "She's not here."

"But she must be. She's the houskeeper-companion."

There was a pause. Then, "Wrong number!"

"But isn't that 26A Walton Street?

There was no answer.

I panicked. "Doesn't Mr Angus Livingstone live there?"

Click, the line went dead.

The voice had hung up.

Five

It was weird. Heather had worked there for over a year. She got jobs as a companion to sick or old people, often travelling abroad with them. Once she went to the South of France. She'd often written about Mr Livingstone. He was a Scottish widower with Multiple Sclerosis - a kind man who had a farm outside Edinburgh and was interested in horses. Her last letter came from his address. What had happened? My panic was increasing, but I controlled it. There had to be a simple answer. The voice on the phone was mistaken. Whoever it was, was new to the job, I persuaded myself. Or else Heather was using her unmarried name of Fitzgerald. Why hadn't I thought of that?

Now the question was whether we should take a taxi there? Or go straight to our jobs in the Cumberland?

I went back to Katie. She was studying a leaflet. "Did you get through?"

I kept my voice calm. "Yes, but I was cut off. Some idiot answered. What're you reading?"

She handed me the leaflet. "A foreign woman gave me this."

WHOM YOU SEEK, YOU WILL FIND HERE was printed on an orange leaflet. In the corner was an address off Piccadilly Circus.

I wadded it up. "She's some religious nut."

My sister grabbed it back. "Don't! It could be useful."

"You're stupid!"

She smoothed out the leaflet. "'Whom you seek, you will find here.' Don't you think that's ironic?"

"Don't use words you don't understand."

She bristled. "*What* don't I understand?'
"Irony."
She reddened in anger. "Well, it's coincidence then. We're looking for someone and we get a message -."
"You mean coincidental."
"That's what I said!"
"You said coincidence!"
"You think you're so clever!"
Next thing she was in tears.
"Look, I'm sorry. I'm getting my period, right?"
"OK."
This is our pact - understanding each other's moods before our periods. But my sister was maddening. She believed in stupid things like fate. It was all Brigid's fault. Because of her, she got hysterical about walking under ladders. Or if a picture fell from the wall, it meant seven years' bad luck. Or if you had thirteen at a dinner, you might die or something. Even tea-leaves in a cup had significance. The two of them even read astrology columns. I believed in science.

She studied the leaflet. "It could be -."

I sighed wearily. I knew she was thinking it was some sort of clue. As well as being superstitious, my sister's a fan of detective novels. Herself and Grandfather read nothing else. They'd retarded her, I always thought. I mean, she once wanted to be a sleuth. "If Heather wanted to give us a message, she'd have met us!"

"What if she *couldn't*?"

"Let's have something to eat," I placated. "Then take a taxi to her job."

We hauled our stuff to the café.

While Katie kept a seat, I queued for food. There was nothing but sandwiches in cardboard packets or breakfast for three pounds each, which we both had.

Has Anyone Seen Heather?

After a feed of rashers, eggs, tea and toast, we felt enormously better. Breakfast's not a bad meal at all. If you eat a big one, you're able to skip lunch.

Katie wanted to check our luggage, but I wouldn't.

"But we'll get tired carrying it round!" she argued.

"No," I said, keeping patience.

"There you go again!"

"Please, Katie, let's not fight?"

She gave in and we followed the signs for taxis. Outside the station a few people were already queuing. When our turn came, Katie clambered excitedly into the big black cab. "They're just like in films."

True, the London taxi's distinctive. And, as it was her first time abroad, it was especially thrilling for her.

"Where to?" the driver shouted back.

I checked our letter. "26A Walton Street."

"Where?" he quizzed again.

"26A Walton Street. Round the corner from Beauchamp Place."

"Let's 'ave that again." He was a cockney.

"It's round the corner from Beauchamp Place."

"Never heard of it!"

Katie nudged me. I knew she imagined we were in some thriller. But this was more like a Kafka story - Wally'd lent me his stories. Or one of my dreams. The woman on the phone had never heard of Heather, and now the street didn't exist.

I held out our letter. "It's written here."

"Let's see!" He reached back, grabbing it. "Y'mean Walton Street! And it's *Beecham* Place!" He sort of swallowed his words like all the cockneys.

"It's French," I argued. "Pronounced *Bow*champ."

He tore through the traffic. "French me arse! You Paddies can't speak the Queen's English."

I'm not patriotic. I've always hated the idea of our

country being a dark Rosaleen sighing and weeping. But that summer changed me. It was an education in the English view of us, Irish. We were like poor relations. Or step-children. Gradually I learnt to ignore insults. But then I answered greenly, "The best English is spoken in Dublin."

"Bleedin' stay there, then! Ye'er all bleedin' IRA!"

I was mad. "We have the best writers and the best actors too."

Then Katie shouted through the partition. "You started it!"

The breaks screeched as he narrowly missed a big red bus.

I mouthed at my sister, "Shut up!"

But she went on angrily, "You invaded our country in 1169!"

He laughed unpleasantly. "You were bleedin' savages, that's why!"

I nudged her, but it was no use.

"You've bullied us for 750 years!"

"Aw, get stuffed!" He slammed the partition shut.

"No way!" Katie shouted back.

We looked at each other then burst out laughing. The IRA were about as remote to us as the Zulus. We only read about the bombing in the North. We saw it as an endless quarrel with no solution. And nothing to do with us. But, like a lot of English people, the taxi-driver knew absolutely nil about Ireland. He lumped us all together as fanatics. But he might overcharge us if we said anything more. Or bring us to the wrong place. So I distracted my sister, pointing out the sights. I knew the area round Marble Arch. And names like Marylebone, Edgeware Road and Park Lane were familiar from Monopoly. Katie stared out the window in a state of high excitement. It was her first time abroad. And although I'd been here before, I'd have been excited too, only for the worry of Heather. Why hadn't she met us?

Walton Street was a small street of tall white houses with steps down to the street. Pont Street criss-crossed with it and Beauchamp Place. And I remember a church on the corner. Our driver stopped in front of number 26A. It looked rich and had a tree growing up from the basement area.

Avoiding eye-contact, we paid and got out.

It took two rings on the bell before a heavy white-coated woman opened the door. She had short tufty red hair and small eyes, blinking behind thick glasses.

"Yes," she said coldly. "What do you want?"

It was the voice on the phone.

"I'm Clare Kelly," I said. And this is my sister Katie."

That didn't seem to mean anything.

I cleared my throat. "We're Heather Kelly's daughters."

She stared, sort of calculatingly.

"She's expecting us," I explained.

"We wired," Katie added.

She still stared.

It was odd.

Then Katie dumped her case, demanding tiredly, "Doesn't our mother work here?"

Then I remembered to say, "She might be using her unmarried name - Fitzgerald?"

Just then a Scottish voice came through a walky-talky grill on the doorframe. "Who is it, Mrs Hanna?"

She leant towards it. "Two girls claiming to be Mrs Kelly's daughters."

"Well, ask them in."

The woman seemed about to shout something back, but didn't. "Certainly, Mr Livingstone."

Has Anyone Seen Heather?

Then she opened the door reluctantly, indicating we were to leave our stuff in the highly polished hall. She showed us into a little ante-room off this. "Wait here."

"She's a crook," Katie whispered, as the door shut.

I ignored my sister, sitting on a chintzy couch. I wasn't in the mood for her lurid imaginings. True, something odd was going on, something I didn't understand. Why had the woman pretended not to know our mother? And she wouldn't have let us in if Mr Livingstone hadn't intervened. But she hadn't actually said where Heather was. Maybe she was here? Maybe she'd walk through the door in a minute and everything'd be OK.

Katie paced the room, examining the ornaments and pictures of racehorses on the walls. The place reeked of money. "Did you notice the scar on her upper lip?"

"Shut up! You're making me nervous."

She sat opposite me. "So you admit there's something fishy?"

Then the door opened.

But it wasn't Heather. The redhaired woman pushed in an old man in a wheelchair. I guessed he was my mother's employer. He wore a red tartan dressing-gown and had thick, black, white-streaked hair and darkish skin. Although sick-looking, he was handsome in an actorish way.

"They might know something, Mr Livingstone," the woman said, looking us over suspiciously.

He smiled weakly. "You must be Clare and Katie. I've heard so much about you girls."

His voice was low and musical.

"Our mother's expecting us," I said.

A sad look flitted across his face. His eyes drooped mournfully like a cocker spaniel's. "I'm afraid the bird has flown, my dears."

"They might be accomplices!" the woman snapped.

What did she mean, "accomplices?" She was like someone heaping coals on Mr Livingstone's uncertainty.

But he heaved a sigh. "Please, Mrs Hanna!"

He wasn't against us. I groped in my bag for her letter. "Our mother wrote, inviting us. Here's the letter."

He glanced at the postmark. "It was posted last week."

I checked: it was.

His gaze moved from one of us to the other. "We haven't seen your mother since then. She left -."

"With a valuable painting!" the woman snapped. "They must know where she is, Mr Livingstone."

He frowned irritably, looking again from one of us to the other.

We stood in shocked silence.

"Perhaps it's some terrible mistake," the old man finally said worriedly shaking his head.

"It's no mistake!" the woman said sharply.

"I was fond of Heather - ah - your mother."

This seemed to anger Mrs Hanna. "Trusting people has got you into this mess!"

What were they were talking about? "Could you explain exactly what our mother is accused of?" I kept my voice calm.

Mr Livingstone's bushy eyebrows met. "A painting is missing. By William Turner."

"It's worth twenty-five thousand pounds," the woman blurted.

I was still puzzled. "What are you saying? That our mother stole it?"

"She wouldn't!" Katie snapped, red with anger.

"I'll admit it's hard to believe." The old man paused.

"Your mother held a position of trust."

"I warned you!" The woman's small eyes glinted madly.

"Mrs Hanna, please!" He looked at us, puzzled, then went on kindly. "You say your mother expected you for the summer?"

I nodded. "She was to meet us at Euston."

He coughed chestily. The cough turned into a spasm, but he finally got his breath. "Excuse me! Well - it seems you know less than we do. I'm sorry we can't be of more help."

"It's OK," I said stupidly. He wasn't a well man.

"Where will you go now?" he asked.

"To the -." But Katie nudged me into silence.

I frowned at her. She was being ridiculous. Heather's employer was no ogre. Honesty was the only way to clear things up. "Our job's live-in," I went on. We're chamberpersons at the Cumberland. We should probably be going."

A smile flitted across his face. "Chamber*persons*?"

I nodded.

He looked quickly at Mrs Hanna. "But can't we offer them refreshments?"

She started to say something, but I shook my head. Her food would stick in our throats. I'd choke on it.

"Well, if you - ah - see your mother, you can tell her that charges will be withdrawn if ..."

Mrs Hanna bristled. "But Mr Livingstone ..."

"If she returns the painting."

Charges. That meant the police were involved. Oh, God, what would we do?

"I'm sure there's a mistake," I said, as we were ushered out.

There had to be a mistake.

Six

The word "charges" had stunned me. Had Mr Livingstone already gone to the police? Probably. We were now back out on the pavement. Although hard and unfriendly, it was better than that house with its atmosphere of sickness and suspicion. But we were sort of dizzy with shock and feeling the lack of sleep. After all we'd been up all night. The accusation was crazy. There had to be an explanation. But, of course, it set Katie off on one of her silly theories. Now she had something real to solve. There was a plot against Heather. And it wasn't in one of her stupid books.

"Mrs Hanna probably stole it!" she whispered, as I figured the direction in which to walk. "She looks like a thief."

I didn't know what to say. I didn't like the look of Mrs Hanna either. But Grandfather always said I was the "sensible" one. I had to keep my head now. If only this was a dream, but it wasn't.

"Come on," I dragged my case towards the corner of Beauchamp Place. There had to be an Underground Station in Knightsbridge. Katie followed me, studying the leaflet she'd been given in the station.

As we passed by shops and restaurants, she said, "Let's go down to Piccadilly."

I thought her crazy. "What for?"

She shrugged. "It's just a feeling."

"You shouldn't give in to your feelings."

I walked on. That's what Sister Martin in school always said. Also, it hadn't done Othello any good. Or our father.

"Please!" she begged.

"No, we're going straight to the Cumberland."

There might be a message there. Why hadn't I thought of that before? Of course, it was obvious. We found our way to the hotel by Underground - the maps were easy to read. By now we were feeling the weight of our luggage, and I was regretting not checking it in. But luckily the Cumberland's entrance was right where we came out at Marble Arch. Revolving doors led us into a luxurious lobby. I left Katie sitting on a round couch with our cases and went to the desk. But we were in the wrong place. This entrance was only for guests. A receptionist directed me to the staff quarters which turned out to be a nearby skyscraper.

In the Housekeeper's Office, a plastic young woman looked us over from behind a huge desk. She flicked through a fat file. "Let me see, Clare and Katharine Kelly. I'm afraid there's no record of your application."

It was a bad dream. "But I got a letter confirming our jobs."

She perused my face. "Do you have it with you?"

Of course, I hadn't.

She shook her head slowly. "Then I'm afraid there's nothing I can do."

I couldn't believe it. First no Heather and now no job.

Katie fiddled nervously with her hair. "We've come all the way from Ireland."

The woman's mouth hardened. "If you'd been employed, you'd be on this list."

It was their mix-up. I'd definitely got the letter. "Could you not give us a job?"

The woman pursed her lips. "Well -." She ran a biro down the list. I could take one of you - on a temporary basis. Whoever is the oldest. I assume you're both sixteen?"

"Yes," I said quickly. Katie had her faked ID. But I couldn't part from my sister. Catching her glance, I knew she felt the same. We fought OK, but we were basically together. Anyway it wasn't practical. She couldn't hang round London on her own. What would she do? Where would she go? No, we'd have to try for jobs elsewhere. I looked at the woman. "We'd prefer to stay together."

"Then, there's nothing I can do."

I shifted awkwardly. Where would we go from here? "Have you any suggestions?"

She frowned officiously. "Do you have any skills?

"Skills?"

"Yes, can you type? Do word processing?

I shook my head. "No."

"Hmm. Well then, you'll just have to try the smaller hotels. There's work in London."

We picked up our stuff to go. "By the way," I asked. "Would there be a message for us? A letter or something?"

She checked through a bundle of letters, shaking her head. "No. And, as we've no record of you, anything that came would be automatically returned to sender."

I asked her to keep all further letters and we left. The Cumberland was our last connection with Heather. How would she find us now, or we her? Also Wally was meant to be phoning me there. We were adrift in a friendless city. Oh, it wasn't exactly outer space, I know, but it felt so to us. Grandfather's predictions were coming true. We'd come from a safe world. A willow-patterned world of clean tablecloths, china cups and two dear old people. But at no time, then or later, did it occur to us to go back to it. We were determined to find Heather somehow. Especially now that she was accused in the wrong.

Has Anyone Seen Heather?

Back in Marble Arch station, Katie was hungry again - she's absolutely always hungry. I've never seen anyone with such an appetite. So we had a pizza in a cafe at the top of Oxford Street. When we got the bill, I checked my money. "How much have you left?"

She rooted in her anorak pocket. Then she tried her jeans. "It must be here."

My heart jumped. Oh, God ... "Try your back pocket!"

She did.

But her purse wasn't there. "What'd you do with it?" I screamed.

She shrugged. "Dunno."

I wanted to hit her. I was unable to speak. But at last I managed to gasp. "How could you?"

She started crying.

I looked round, embarassed. People were looking. "Please stop ... I'm sorry." I was always being mean to her.

"You made me take it out of my rucksack!"

It was true. Someone had picked her pocket.

Things were going so wrong. "You'll come to no good in London," Grandfather's voice said in my head. Well, he was turning out to be right. But no good would come of fighting either. 'One for all and all for one,' was one of Heather's maxims.

"I'm sorry," I whispered, "it was my fault."

This appeased her somewhat. After paying we'd only fifteen pounds left. But it was better than nothing. Maybe we'd get jobs that afternoon. As we'd nowhere to stay, they had to be live-in in central London. So that tied us down to the hotel world - unless we could get work as Domestics. I bought an *Evening Standard* and studied the Hotels and Catering columns. There was one for chamberstaff, so I rang it on spec from Marble

Arch station. It was the Mount Royal. The jobs were gone, but the housekeeper suggested we try the Imperial at Lancaster Gate.

They said to come for interview the day after next. But at least we had an interview. And maybe our luck would change and we'd get the jobs. But it meant we had two whole days to use up. How were we going to manage till then? When I told Katie all she could say was, "Great, let's go down to Piccadilly."

You see what my sister's like. She gets hold of an idea like a terrier gets hold of a bone. She just won't let it go.

"No," I said. "First, we find a bed for tonight."

I rang a few bed and breakfasts. One woman asked me where I came from. When I said Ireland, she hung up rudely. Another place was £48 for a double room. Imagine? Anyhow they were full. There was no room in the inn. What were we to do? I'd heard of Irish students sleeping rough in London, but that idea frightened me. I knew there was an Irish Centre somewhere, but didn't know where. I was panicking again, but I couldn't. I had to look after Katie.

"Let's go back to Euston and check in our luggage," I said cheerfully. I picked Euston because of Heather. Maybe she'd turn up the next morning? Maybe she'd mixed up the days. Why hadn't I thought of that?

"Can we go to Piccadilly then?"

I nodded vaguely.

We took the Underground again. As we zoomed through the airless tunnels, I kept thinking of Wally's advice to think cosmically. "Pegasus, Pisces, Aquarius, Capricornus, Virgo," I whispered the names of the constellations to myself. A human being is nothing compared to the immensity of space, I told myself. Nothing. We're microscopic ants. Our life is the dance of a butterfly. Why had I panicked? Heather was bound to turn up. She'd be there the next morning. We could spend the night at Euston. What did it matter if you didn't sleep for one night of your life?

Back at the station, we checked in our stuff. Then I suggested we look for a park. We could lie on the grass there and pretend to be sunbathing. Then we could get rest which was badly needed. After that we could go to Piccadilly. We found a small park - London's full of them. I don't remember the name, but it was near the station and a bit like Merrion Square. The gate was locked as we climbed in over the railings.

"It's great to sit down," Katie said, throwing herself down on the grass. In a minute she was asleep.

I was determined to stay awake to guard her. But fell asleep too.

When I awoke there was a boy staring down at me. He had brilliant blue eyes, bad skin and red hair. He was lost in a big ragged overcoat and had a little spotted dog on a lead - a mongrel.

I sat up rubbing my eyes. It took me a minute to remember where I was. Thank God, Katie was still beside me.

"Had a good kip?" he said in an Irish accent.

"I - I fell asleep." I shook Katie awake, slowly remembering how awful everything was.

"What time is it?" she asked, rubbing her eyes.

He looked at a watch. "Seven o'clock."

"Morning or evening?"

"Evening!" He rubbed his face. "On the lamb or something?"

"No," I said. "We've come to London to work." I told him about our interview the day after tomorrow.

He sat down beside us, cuddling the dog in his lap. "It's not safe to sleep in parks."

"We couldn't find a place," I said guiltily.

He cuddled his dog. "I'm squatting in Kilburn. Come up there if you like."

"No thanks," I said quickly. I could see Katie was interested.

"Give us the address," she said.

He did and we chatted for a while. He told us his name was Frank and he made twenty-six pounds a day begging. Imagine? That it was a waste of time to work. And that he'd teach us how if we didn't get the jobs. I pictured our grandfather's face.

"What do you do with all that money?" I asked, thinking he could at least afford a better coat.

"Buy food for Spot here." At this the dog licked him.

Frank was the first nice person we met in London. He showed us a wide spot in the railings and we all squeezed out. Then he walked back to Euston with us, telling us to watch out for the police. That they were on the lookout for teenage runaways. And that they particularly didn't like the Irish. Because of the troubles in the North, the English police picked on the Irish all the time. I knew about the Guildford Four and the Birmingham Six who'd been in jail for years. At Holyhead we'd been stopped, getting off the boat. But when we said we were meeting our mother, they let us go. Our new friend now advised us to move if spotted by a policeman, and if asked, to say we were meeting a train.

We had a sandwich in the café and settled down on two hard chairs in the middle of the crowded station. It was a friendly enough place and familiar to us by now. I was feeling better. A station can supply all your needs - except a bed. There were a few students about and a few down and out types. All night long we could hear the rumble of the Underground trains. Like some monster's tummy. I read my book on Sartre and Katie listened to her walkman. As it got later, the station got quieter and Katie fell asleep sitting up.

The night passed quite quickly. In the early morning, I noticed two police patrolling, a man and a woman. The woman saw us and came over. Oh, God.

"Are you waiting for a train?" she asked nicely enough.

I nodded. Luckily I didn't give my emotions away by blushing. "We're meeting our mother."

"What train is she arriving on?" she quizzed, looking me over sharply.

"She's coming from Holyhead. It's due in soon."

"From Dun Laoghaire?" she pronounced this in a funny English way.

I said yes.

"You're very early. It's only 5 o'clock."

"I thought it best to be early," I answered quickly. "We got a lift here. It was cheaper to take it."

This just came to me and seemed to satisfy her. And at that moment a message came through on her walkie-talkie. She spoke into it for a minute, ending up with "over and out." It was just like the TV.

"Well, be careful," she warned and went back to her companion.

I was a bundle of nerves. My mouth had gone completely dry. Luckily Katie never woke up. She'd only say something to give the game away.

At last the boat train came. We went to meet it, in case the police were watching. But they weren't around and neither was Heather. It was just like yesterday morning with the crowds gradually increasing on their hurried way to work. Everyone in the world had a place to go, except us. I was aching in every limb and decided to try again for a cheap bed and breakfast. I couldn't spend another night awake.

But first we went for a cup of tea and another sandwich. And then something good happened. Maybe guardian angels do exist. Maybe they're on this earth in disguise. Ours was called Bonnie and wore the American uniform of blue jeans, an Aran sweater and Nike tennis shoes. She had long blonde hair and brown freckled skin and sat at the table beside us. Somehow we got talking. You know the way it happens with Americans. They're so friendly and nice. She told us she'd just finished a London semester from the University of California. So when she heard we were looking for a cheap place to stay for the night, she said, "Try Mrs O'Reilly in Baker Street. She's only ten pounds a night and she never turns anyone away."

So I rang. At first a woman's voice said they were full, but I pleaded.

"All right, come over and I'll squeeze you in."

We were saved.

Seven

The hostel was a mad house. It was packed with American students. Some of them actually slept on the floor, which was strewn with their empty sleeping bags. As we didn't have any, we were allowed to share the bottom half of a bunk for five pounds each, including breakfast.

It was for nothing. Only we weren't allowed to go to bed till that evening and it was now only the morning. But the relief of dumping our stuff and having a place to sleep put us into better humour. Ignoring our tiredness, we went in search of the famous home of Sherlock Holmes, 221B Baker Street.

My sister was mad with excitement. But, as I'd heard, it turned out to be a bank - the Abbey National Building Society. People were walking in and out mundanely. Katie peered in the window. "Pity he isn't alive now."

"He never was, dummy!"

She looked taken aback. "I know that! ... we can still apply his methods."

I groaned inwardly. My sister was mental. Grandfather had reared her on Sherlock Holmes and other detective stories. Apart from *A Hundred and One Dalmations*, they were the only books she'd read. As a result, she saw things in black and white. People were either baddies like Cruella de Vil, or goodies like Sherlock Holmes. Despite her skill in art, the nuns in school worried about her English. One teacher claimed she might have a form of dyslexia. I thought it'd help to try more serious books. I mean they might mature her. Things like hounds baying on moors were too much. They didn't reflect reality. Or so I thought. I know better now. Our summer was to change my mind forever about life's possibilities. As I said, anything can happen, 'Enry 'Iggins. Anything. But that lesson was in the future. Then I could only be irritated by Katie's remark.

She was unfolding her leaflet. "Can we go to Piccadilly?"

"No."

"Please!"

I read the leaflet again. Because of the wording, "Whom you seek, you will find here," she was convinced it was some sort of omen. Some message to go to Piccadilly. It was cracked. I thought she'd been affected by all that happened, like people are shell-shocked in war. Or people dying of thirst see mirages in the desert. After all, we were strangers in a strange city. She could be suffering from alienation, or disorientation, or depersonalization, or one of those things Wally was always going on about.

"Let's go to the National Gallery," I said. "You've always wanted to go there." Sometimes you have to get round Katie, rather than thwart her dead-on. She's like our Dad in being hasty, which is probably why they clashed so violently.

Her face set stubbornly now. I knew that look.

"We can see Van Gogh's *Sun Flowers*."

"OK. But then I'm going to Piccadilly." And she headed in the direction of an underground station.

We found the National Gallery and spent several hours there, wandering tiredly from room to room. I can't really remember any of the paintings, except Van Gogh's *Sun Flowers*. I stood for ages in front of those fiery hopeful beautiful colours. How had he done it? Would I ever do anything with my life? In the end I went to look for Katie and found her sitting boredly on a bench. "I thought you liked paintings!"

"I don't! I'm going to Piccadilly." And she charged to the door.

So I followed. What else could I do? My sister has a will of her own, she always has had. As I couldn't restrain her, I had to humour her whims. Otherwise I'd lose control of her completely. I'd lose my authority as older sister. Besides, she might get lost. Or do something stupid.

Has Anyone Seen Heather?

When we got there, it was evening rush hour. Except for the motley group of people who hung around the Statue of Eros, all of London was heading homeward. Pedestrians thronged the pavements. Cars honked. Red buses hurtled down Shaftesbury Avenue like rockets. There were cafés, tourists, tramps, theatres and cinemas. Huge ads flashed for COCA-COLA, CARLSBERG and SANYO, for the SUN ALLIANCE and LONDON ASSURANCE GROUP.

While Katie went to check the address on her leaflet, I sat on the steps by the Statue of Eros, taking it all in. We were living life, or would be if only we could find Heather. London was like the centre of the world, and huge. Yet it was only a capital of a small country on a small planet. There were mountains on the moon, phases of Venus, spots on the sun and satellites of Jupiter. Imagine, the gravity of Jupiter is over three hundred times the strength of earth ... I tried to think cosmically, but the thought of light years made me dizzy.

Instead I sorted out some things in my head. We were on our own for the first time in our lives. So far we'd been with our grandfather and parents. One life was the opposite to the other. Grandfather treated us like children. I mean, he'd never give us a note to miss school, while Heather kept us home for company. But Grandfather wanted to save us. He thought our parents beyond salvation. He was always running them down. It wasn't fair to lump them both together. Heather didn't drink. Oh, she didn't eat sometimes, I know. And took uppers to diet - which she gave to us when she wanted the house cleaned. They were speed really and made us zoom around. But Grandfather didn't know this. He'd have a fit if he did. He believed in food like a religion. And constantly blamed Heather for not cooking properly. She bought everything frozen. I mean, even chips. Yet we missed her cooking so much. Even her spaghetti, which was awful really - a bottle of tomato ketchup over pasta. She was somewhere in this huge haystack. But where?

I watched Katie's red anorak disappear under an arch in the direction of the Regent Palace Hotel. You had to give her her head. When she was given a Bible or something, she'd be satisfied. We could then go back to the hostel and sleep. First she talked to a man. Then she walked on and stopped another. I knew she was asking directions.

My mind wandered back to Heather. Where was she? Was she not eating again? Would I now know what to do? Once I found her in the kitchen, trying to gas herself because Dad was having an affair with another woman. I stopped her and rang Grandfather. He sent Heather to a posh hospital out in Lucan. Oh, she seemed to get better for a while. But the summer I was twelve and Katie eleven, she disappeared completely.

What happened was this: Grandfather had sent us to Irish College in Donegal. But after a week, Heather wrote, saying she'd left Daddy. I just stayed at the college. It was a miserable month. When we came home, Daddy looked after us. But he drank all the time and consequently lost a part in a play at the Gate Theatre. He kept fighting with us. Once Katie cheeked him so he hit her. She had bruises everywhere. I rang Grandfather, so he came and got us. But Dad found us and came banging on the door,

"Give me back my children, you stupid old fart!"

"Go away, or I'll call the police!" Grandfather said.

But Dad kicked the door, roaring, "You bloody old bastard!"

Has Anyone Seen Heather?

It was terrifying.

Grandfather finally rang the police, so he went away. The next thing the ISPCC called to see if we were OK - neighbours had reported our father. They threatened to prosecute him unless he promised not to come again. Then Heather wrote, asking Grandfather to keep us.

We'd been there ever since. When Grandfather runs Dad down, it really upsets me. He says things like, "Of course your mother fell for a handsome face." And, "Your father's a cad." And, "You never know where Americans have come from." I wanted to defend him then, but I couldn't. Grandfather forgets he's our father, for God's sake. He wasn't all bad. For one thing, he was a dedicated artist. Maybe the violence wasn't his fault. He'd been drafted into the US army and had bad experiences in Vietnam. Then he came to Trinity where he'd acted in Players. Our parents met there when my mother was at a play - she was in UCD, but had friends in Trinity. Oh, why had things turned out so badly? I'll never be able to forget him banging the door. I'll never forget the pain in his voice. Why did he drink? I had begged him not to once, but he'd just said, raising a cynical eyebrow. "Always be drunk, Clare." It was the saying of some stupid French poet he liked. He was always quoting poetry. "It's no go my poppet, it's no go my honey love," was another favourite line of his. I missed my Dad, but I'll never forgive him for hitting Heather. Or Katie. Never. I should never have gone to Irish College. I should never have left Heather alone with him. What if she'd disappeared again? Thinking of the row with Daddy, tears came into my eyes. Although he'd given me my love for theatre, I hated him. I did. He'd driven Heather away. Thanks to him, I was a feminist. I took out my wallet and studied Heather's photo. She had a bony face, blue eyes and blonde shoulder-length hair - dyed. It was a carefree face, despite her unhappy marriage. Stupidly, I looked around, perusing every woman's face in the crowd. Heather was somewhere in London. She could easily be walking right here. Oh, I didn't really expect to see her. I know that. But everything was so unreal. The old brain must've been affected by tiredness or something.

When I looked again, Katie was missing.

She's probably found the place, I thought. She'll be back in a minute.

Then I saw her in the distance.

Being marched up Regent Street by a policeman!

I tore across the street into the crowds. Why had I let her go by herself? Where was he taking her? And why? Had she done something? Was she being arrested for being Irish?

Finally I caught them.

The policeman was gripping her arm.

"Leave my sister alone." My breath was gone.

He towered over both of us, glaring from under a black helmet. "I'm taking her to the station."

Katie was white with fear. Suddenly I could feel all my love for her. Why does it take a crisis to recognise your true feelings?

"I - I didn't do anything!" she said.

"She was soliciting," he said grimly.

I was speechless. What did he mean? "Soliciting?"

He pulled his chin strap into place. "I'm taking her into protective custody."

He dragged her on.

Then it dawned on me: Did he think she was a prostitute?

"Wait!" I gasped. "She was only checking an address."

But he wouldn't stop.

Has Anyone Seen Heather?

I ran to keep up. "Katie, where's the leaflet?"
She managed to pass it to me.
"Look, someone gave us this at Euston!"
He snapped it from me.

While he read it, I explained that our mother wasn't there to meet us. So my sister thought the leaflet was some sort of omen. It sounded idiotic, which it was. But I stammered on, that we had interviews for a job the next morning and were booked into a hostel for the night.

He was totally unmoved and completely different to the policewoman in Euston.

"Do you have any identification?"
"What?"
"An ID. Passport. Anything to identify you."

I gave him our faked IDs. If he knew Katie's real age, he might take her into care.

She was now sobbing loudly.

He returned them, grinning sarcastically. "Your sister is really seventeen?"

I nodded.

"She doesn't look it!"
"I am ... " she mumbled.
"Well, it's still illegal to solicit!"

Oh, God, I prayed. Please help. In moments of stress, my agnosticism completely disappears. It's amazing. I started a prayer to Our Lady in my head, a prayer which, according to Brigid, is never known to fail. "Remember, oh most gracious Virgin Mary, that never was it known ... " Then, getting my breath, I said aloud, "Listen, we didn't know it was wrong to ask directions."

He rubbed his chin, perplexed.

"We're from Ireland."

He laughed grimly. "I'd gathered that." He looked us

both over. "Are you runaways?"

"No!"

"Well, how much money have you got?"

I showed him my remaining money.

"That won't take you far!"

"But we have an interview at the Imperial Hotel in the morning."

He hesitated - this seemed to impress him.

"Please, let her go!" I was nearly crying.

He looked from one to the other, inwardly deciding.

It was an eternity.

Finally he spoke into a walkie-talkie, calling a squad car.

We waited in dread.

There was a siren and a car screeched up and we were told to get in.

He said something to the driver, then turned sternly to us. "We'll drive you back to your hostel. But I'm warning you, we pick up kids like your sister all the time. If she's caught again, she'll be taken into care. A faked ID won't help!"

As we zoomed across London in the squad car, I was afraid to protest. The word "care" scared me. It was a word I knew. A social worker from the ISPCC had once called on Grandfather, suggesting the same thing. I was filled with dread. Life was so unfair. What kind of a country had we come to? Katie was only asking directions. But we were free, that's all that mattered. Things would work out. Heather would get in touch. We had a place to sleep and the hope of a job. And there was no point in blaming Katie. It was my fault for letting her go on her own.

The police left us at the hostel. It was now full and rang with the laughter of Americans. Katie flopped into the bottom of the bunk assigned to us. Some of the girls in the room queued for the bathroom. I joined the end.

"Hi," a voice called from across the room. "You made it!"

It was Bonnie, our guardian angel from Marble Arch. She had a towel wrapped around her head. It reminded me of our last breakfast with Grandfather, when he'd called Katie the Ayatollah. I missed him now too. He'd know what to do about Heather. Why do you never appreciate people 'till it's too late?

I waved.

She came over. "We're going for a pint later. Like to join us?"

"I'm afraid we're - tired," I said. Although I'd sworn never to drink, I was quite glad she'd asked. Nobody had ever asked me to go to a pub before. It was proof I looked older.

She looked snubbed. "Well, maybe another time."

I nodded tiredly. We had no money and no hope of money until we were working. And even if we were allowed into a pub, we'd left the carefree world of youth. We were in a different country. And like Halley's comet, going the opposite way to the universe. I didn't speak to anyone else. I just climbed into our ten-pound bunk and slept a head-to-foot sleep of exhaustion.

Eight

I had bad dreams again that night. I dreamt that Katie and I were standing outside this big house, waiting to get in. It was a house in Dublin where our parents once had a flat. No matter how hard we knocked, they wouldn't open the door. It was terrible. And when I awoke, Heather was still missing. As the occupant of the top bunk moved, I stared despairingly at the criss-cross wires above me. Where was Heather? Sleep hadn't knitted up the ravelled sleeve. There was still the problem of finding her. What were we to do? On top of everything, I had my period.

I got up and went to the bathroom. Then it came to me. Perhaps Heather thought we were travelling today. Maybe she'd be at Euston, I'd go back one last time. It was near enough to Baker Street.

So I got dressed and went, while Katie slept.

But of course, Heather wasn't there. Hopelessly, I paced the platforms, almost getting swept away by the crowds. It was crazy. In the end I put a notice up on the police board, under the rapist's photograph.

HEATHER KELLY. WE ARE IN LONDON. CONTACT US AT THE IMPERIAL HOTEL, LANCASTER GATE. CLARE.

We weren't definitely working there yet. But if not, I'd ask them to take a message. Katie was still asleep when I got back. I had an awful job getting her up. But after a lot of grumbling, she did. Then we stood in line with the other students for a huge breakfast of rashers, eggs, beans and chips. We felt better then and arranged to leave our stuff until the job was definite. Then took the Underground to Lancaster Gate.

The Imperial Hotel was off the Bayswater Road. We found it easily enough and were shown into the head housekeeper's cubby-hole of an office. Miss King was the first of the oddities we met there. She was a bearded giantess with massive breasts which seemed to join in the middle like one huge mountain. That morning she wore a black uniform dress with a frilly white hat and collar like a Victorian hospital matron. I told Katie to let me do the talking. I explained we needed jobs, and waited nervously.

She inspected us over half-moon glasses. "Have you previous hotel experience?"

"Yes," I lied. "I was a chamberperson in Dublin."

She sniffed. "In this hotel we use the Queen's English. And we employ maids. Not persons."

I reddened. She wasn't very nice. Her cold fishy eyes reminded me of the headmistress in some horrible school story. Or Mrs Thatcher - she obviously had the same Empire complex and right wing values. She had a weird military streak and addressed us by our surnames, although that wasn't the worst.

"Do you have a reference?"

This threw me. "It was last summer. I lost it. I've worked in a cinema since."

She pursed her lips. "Dear me. You do move round, don't you?"

"I'm a student. We're both at school."

She grimaced. "Students? I was looking for permanent staff."

"We'll stay till the end of August."

Her swan-like bosom heaved indecisively. "But you Irish never keep your word."

We looked at each other.

She forced a smile. "But I suppose you're not as bad as our darker friends."

We were actually supposed to laugh at this. I might as well mention her worst fault was racism. She hated the black staff. I couldn't believe it. London was the most racist, sexist, coldest place in the world, but she was the worst person we met. I mean, what planet were we on? Had Martin Luther King died in vain? He was my favourite character from all of history. Things were terrible back then. But for God's sake, we were now conquering space. Had it taken four billion years to produce people like Miss King? Normally I wouldn't dream of even talking to such a person, never mind working for them. But then I was desperate.

She studied a file.

The wait was agonising.

You have to compromise in this world. It was one thing I learnt from that summer. We'd have said anything, agreed to anything for the job. Finally she snapped the file shut. "Well, beggars can't be choosers. Can you start immediately?"

"Yes! But we have to get our stuff."

It was settled we'd start the next morning.

We were saved.

Although a West End Hotel, the Imperial was Dickensian. It was full of weirdos. The oddest was a gay chef called Jennifer, who wore women's clothes. Oh, I didn't think there was anything wrong with being gay. I'm not antediluvian like Grandfather. Why should everyone be straight? I just thought it odd that Jennifer wanted to be a woman when he obviously hated them - he yelled at us all the time. It was terrifying. And the night porter was a male chauvinist sex-fiend. But the Spanish assistant housekeeper, Miss Lopez, was nice enough, although a real religious maniac. The rest were some very surly Irish - but again I'm going too far ahead. Things were only revealed by degrees.

The pay was over sixty pounds a week, plus keep. To us it was riches, but we learnt quickly how London gobbled money. We slept in two camp beds in a bathroom at the top of the house with horrible creepy crawlies coming out of the drain. God, they were awful. The only other furniture was a table with a phone. At six every morning, the night porter rang us with, "Wakie, wakie!" He always made some sexual suggestion like, "Had we had a hard night?" It was disgusting. Before breakfast we had to take the guests tea or coffee - disguised Nescafé, actually. Then, after staff breakfast in the hotel kitchen, we started on the rooms assigned by Miss King.

Her name suited her. She ruled over her bedraggled kingdom like a potentate. The cleaning staff lined up outside the office with bucket and mop in hand. There were a gang of Irish girls who, like us, lived in - they had a flat somewhere near the hotel to which we were never invited. All the rest, mostly black women or Indians, lived out. We loved their cheerfulness, but we clashed with our own countrywomen. They hated us. But it was mutual. I hated their bad language. Maybe I'm a prude. Wally says I am, but I can't help it - my Dad had called Heather names. Names I could never bear to repeat.

Mary Murphy was given the task of showing us the job. She had red hair, dirty finger nails, bad BO and eyes like two cigarette holes. She was supposed to come round with us for the first day. But instead disappeared, leaving us to do all the work. So we ended up exhausted.

Afterwards, I found her smoking in the linen

cupboard between the stacks of towels. "We're finished," I said.

She flicked back her long red hair and stubbed out a cigarette. "You have to be inspected."

Then she walked sexily into one of the rooms. Running her nicotined finger over the sink, she snapped. "That won't pass!"

I asked why. I'd scrubbed it carefully.

She stood with her arms akimbo. "Cos it's wet."

"Wet?"

"Yes. It's meant to be dry. Dry all the sinks and baths with a used towel like this."

So we had to go round again, drying everything. It was crazy. They'd be wet as soon as people used them again.

But after that first day, Katie and I worked together. We were only responsible for ourselves. All day we scrubbed baths, made beds and hoovered acres of carpets. It's amazing what goes on backstage in hotels. It'd put you off them for life. I'm not joking either. Everything was the epitome of sleaze. We soon learned useful tricks. For instance, it wasn't always necessary to change the sheets. Or hoover. Or clean the baths too carefully. But despite shortcuts, the work was killing. We were exhausted. But proud of ourselves as well. Despite Grandfather's predictions, we were coping. And all on our own. The pity was, he couldn't see us. Then maybe he'd realise we weren't infants.

I sent him and Brigid a card:

Arrived safely. Heather arranged jobs at a different hotel. All going well. Address above. We've done some sightseeing. Heather sends best wishes. See you soon. Love in tons, Clare and Katie.

Then I rang the Cumberland with our new address,

asking them to send on letters. Or tell anyone who called where we were - I was expecting to hear from Wally too. He'd get in touch there. And every day we expected Heather to contact us. Somehow she'd see the notice at Euston. Or ring Grandfather. Looking back, it was wishful thinking. But we were sort of disorientated and lived in a limbo of expectation. I think we just blanked out Mr Livingstone's accusation. It couldn't be true. When Heather turned up, which she would, one day soon, everything'd be OK. Our mother hadn't done anything wrong. It was psychological denial, Wally later told me. And I suppose he was right. He's an expert on things like that. And knows absolutely everything.

Nine

After a week, I rang the Cumberland again. But there was still no word of Heather. Maybe she'd rung Grandfather. But I was afraid to find out. My voice might give me away. And if Grandfather discovered Heather hadn't met us, he'd only say "I told you so. See how unreliable your mother is!" The wedge between them'd be driven deeper. Also he'd come right over. He'd say we were too young to be on our own. And take us home. So the days passed.

I suppose I should've gone to the police. But our experience at Piccadilly had frightened me. I've always had this obsession about Katie being taken into care. It was something that haunted me since the row with Dad when social workers had called on Grandfather. Maybe subconsciously I thought there was some truth in Mr Livingstone's accusation. Heather was flighty. She was capable of acting irresponsibly. I mean, going to too many parties. In Dublin I could look after her. But she was lost now. How could we find her? We didn't have any money. And even if we had, how do you find someone? Where do you begin? We were no Scarlet Pimpernels. If you don't believe me, try it. Just try, 'Enry 'Iggins. Find someone in a huge impersonal city.

Also we were flattened by the work. Grandfather always said if you worked with your hands, you learnt the value of an education. And he was dead right. When we came off duty about three, we just flopped into bed. Then wandered aimlessly up and down the Bayswater Road, with its endless mechanical traffic, until it was time to turn down the beds for the night. The duty, by the way, was split. We only seemed to have so much time off.

Also the work was embarassing. Sometimes people never got up. Or let us in when they were scantily clad, especially in the evenings. Sometimes they'd be still in bed, when they were meant to be enjoying London. I couldn't understand it. Why come on a holiday and spend your time in bed? What could possibly take all day?

One evening a man got locked out of his room. He looked really funny. He was naked except for a towel round his pot belly

Seeing me at the end of the corridor, he gesticulated wildly. "Hey! You there!"

"Don't worry," I came up, smiling and jangling my

Has Anyone Seen Heather?

keys. "I'll let you in."

He was a foreigner. Oldish, about forty. With a handsome baby face and floppy pepper and salt hair. His irritation changed to amusement. He spoke to me in broken English. "I am looking for de ice. But dere are no macheen."

I unlocked his door. "Ring room service. They'll send it up."

"But you help?" There was a flirtatious look in his eye.

"I'm the chamberstaff. I do the beds."

He tut-tutted under his breath. "You Engleesh, you are all the same! You weel not oblige."

"I'm not English. And I'm not allowed into the bar." I headed off down the corridor.

"But you must do my bed!" he called petulantly.

"I'll come back later." I thought he'd want to put on some clothes.

But he crimsoned with anger. "No! Now, please! Now! What ees your name, pleese?"

"Clare Kelly."

"Mees Kelly, do my room!"

"It's Ms Kelly." I went back to his room, turning down the covers and slapping the pillows. Why couldn't people do this for themselves? And why did he wander around half naked. It was disgusting.

He watched me with a look of satisfaction, tucking his towel around his waist. "So you are not Engleesh. What are you then? Scottish?"

I said I was Irish.

"Ah!" Then he sat on his bed, singing an American song, *"I dr-e-am of Jeanie with the light brown hair ... "* You have such lovlee songs. And such a literature. Have you heard of James Joyce?"

"Of course!" We'd read one of his short stories in

English class - "Araby."

He nodded knowingly. "You will be a teacher?"

I shrugged. "I'm still at school."

He laughed. "All the Irish, dey are teachers or nurses."

He chatted on for a few minutes. In the end I rang the porter for his damn ice. After all, he had said nice things about Ireland. And recognised us as a cut above the other staff - it was snobbish of me, but they were so awful to us. I decided he was jokey and really rather nice.

Over the next few mornings the Frenchman became quite friendly, lingering while we did the room. He even gave Katie a record of U2 he'd found on the boat on the way over. He told us he was on a sabbatical and looking for a flat near the British Museum where he was doing research. Later he was going to Cornwall. We chatted about James Joyce, on whom he was some kind of expert. But he liked Conan Doyle too and told Katie to go to a pub called The Sherlock Holmes.

"She has the pledge," I shouted over the hoover.

"A leetle wine is good," he joked.

She looked out of the bathroom. "I'll have a coke."

I imagined his life of civilized learning, with wine and coffee à la Sartre.

But I was wrong. Dead wrong.

One evening there was no answer to my knock and no *Do Not Disturb* sign on his door. So I went in.

He was lying on top of a woman.

Both were starkers.

She saw me and screamed.

"*Merde!*" he shouted, jumping up.

I just stood there. "Eh - sorry!"

He grabbed a robe and came for me. So I retreated quickly, running down the corridor.

But he caught me near the lift.

"Stupid beetch!" He danced up and down with rage, yelling. "I have you fired! I have you fired!"

It was no name to call a woman. No matter what.

Ten

It's amazing how you can like someone. But then they do something which makes them repulsive. My impression of the professor had changed utterly. From being handsome, he was now frightening. Everything about him was sinister. His wild hair was uncivilised and the grey stubble on his chin decadent. I cast aside all my imagined scenarios for his cultured and highly superior life.

He obviously felt the same way about us. He had the hall porter ring us to come down to reception the next day and then demanded the U2 record back.

"It's in our room," I mumbled.

He danced in temper. "I want it back!"

I looked at Katie.

"I'll get it," she said, running back upstairs to our room.

It was mental. He couldn't really want the record. I was afraid to stay near him, but the hall porter was there. When Katie came back with the record about five minutes later, he grabbed it rudely and stormed off.

From then on, he snubbed us. It wasn't fair. I didn't know anyone was in the room. No one was meant to be. It was a mistake, that's all. Of course, we got told off and were assigned to a different floor. Mary Murphy was given our beat. She'd lorded it over us ever since that first day. Like the other Irish staff, she shunned our company. Oh, maybe it was our fault. Maybe we were unfriendly to her. But she never spoke, and when she did every second word was unmentionable.

Then our unpopularity came to a head. It was at breakfast about the end of our first week. The staff were always served out greasy fries by Jennifer in the hotel kitchen. It was a weird name for a man and he was weird: eye-make up, dyed blond hair and high-heeled boots. He walked with a mincing female step and waved his hands like flippers. I suppose he was fed-up with being a man. And who could blame him?

That morning I was eating at the table, while Katie queued for food. I heard her say, "I'd like a poached egg, please."

"It's fried or nothing, ducks!" Jennifer screamed from behind the counter.

Katie politely declined his blobs of grease.

"You paddies are all the same! Here! Poach 'em yourself!" Then he threw two raw eggs at my sister.

This brought exclamations from the other staff. But Mary Murphy, who was sitting opposite me, giggled. It was desperately mean. How could she?

I ran to my sister with a paper napkin. "It's Ok."

She was crying. Eggy goo slimed down her face.

I turned on Jennifer. "You shouldn't have done that!"

"What do you intend doing about it, ducks?" His voice rose several octaves.

"Report you!" I heard myself say.

"Why don't you go and fuck yourself!"
I was speechless.
The silence was broken by a hiss as he threw a packet of rashers onto the huge hot plate.
No one took our side, not even the kitchen porters.
Mary giggled again.
I was red to the roots. I wanted to kill her. But there was nothing I could do. So I took my sister upstairs to our bedroom. The incident seemed to focus all our unhappiness about Heather. Why was everything so awful? Where was she? How would we find her?
But you can't let people walk on you. For the moment there was nothing we could do about finding Heather. But we could report Jennifer. So before starting our chores that morning, I knocked on Miss King's door.
She peered at me over a clipboard. "What is it, Kelly?"
I told her what had happened.
Her face registered nothing. "Well, chef can be temperamental. Poached eggs are difficult. You're not exactly guests, are you?"
I wanted to say we're human beings, but muttered, "He shouldn't have thrown eggs."
"Your sister shouldn't have demanded them. It comes of forgetting your place."
My stomach knotted with anger. "We have rights."
Her massive bosom heaved. "You're only the cleaning staff."
"But we're -."
She shook her head. "I'm surprised at you girls. Usually our black friends stir up trouble."
Her remark shocked me into silence.
"Get back to your work now!"
"But it's ..."

She took off her glasses. "I could replace you two in the morning,"

I wanted to shout, "Do that!"

"Chefs are a different matter." And she nodded dismissively over her glasses.

In the hotel pecking order, chamberpersons were scum - to staff and guests alike. No one ever left a tip and no one took our side against Jennifer. Later that day we met the Spanish Assistant Housekeeper, who just shrugged and told us to forget it too.

Cosmically it was nothing, I know. One ant upsets another, that's all it was. But it was a turning point. We decided to leave. The problem was other jobs. In our time off, we were too tired to look. Never mind do anything definite about Heather. So for the moment, there was nothing to do but take it. Where would we find another job? London was full of unemployed Irish. You saw them sometimes in parks. Young people sitting in circles and smoking cigarettes. I knew they were Irish by their accents. The thought of having no money and no place to go was too much for me. We were sort of suspended in time. And lived in an anxious state of dread. I was even getting angry with Heather. How could she treat us like this? How could she be so inconsiderate? Maybe we should pack up and go home. Maybe she didn't really want us. It certainly looked like it. But then other thoughts chased out the bad ones. She could need us. She could be bad with nerves again, not eating. Or in hiding from Mr Livingstone. She could have done it.

Katie was all for action, while I wanted to wait and see. In *War and Peace*, a Russian general said if you don't know what to do, do nothing. He was describing Napoleon's invasion. Our problems were nothing like facing a French army but, we were stuck in the same rut of inaction. In the end I rang Grandfather. But Heather hadn't been in touch with him either. Luckily Brigid answered the phone.

"Clare, dear, how are you?" she said in a delighted voice.

Suddenly I loved her. "Great. How are you?"

"Fine." Then she lowered her voice tragically. "Except, you know I'm a prisoner here."

I changed the subject. "How's Grandad?"

"He's worrying about you girls!"

"Well, there's no need!"

"How's darling Heather?"

"She's great, Brigid," I lied. "She got us other jobs. Much nicer than the Cumberland. A family hotel."

"Well, I hope they realise you're nice girls, from a good home?"

"Yes, Brigid." I pictured Miss King's face if I said this. "How's Yuppie?"

"Oh, naughty as ever."

She loved to get on to her dog and talked about him for the rest of the time. Luckily I didn't give anything away. I gave her our address, asking her to forward any letters.

Where was Heather? Why hadn't she phoned Grandfather? Although they didn't usually speak, they had to sometimes.

It was a miserable puzzle.

One night in bed, Katie was listening to her music. It was *Missing You*, by Enya.

I was trying to read, but the music made me too lonely. It seemed to be doing the same to Katie, because she snapped it off saying, "Do you think Heather'll ever get in touch?"

I didn't know. Heather didn't know where we were. But I said, "It's only a matter of time."

My sister sighed heavily. "Do you think it's her anorexic?"

"Anorexia. Maybe, but it doesn't affect your memory."

"What's that?"

"What's what?"

"When your memory's affected?"

"Amnesia. It happens in films." I'd seen *Random Harvest* where a man came back from the war and didn't even recognise his own wife. Just at the last scene Grandfather made me go to bed. I was really enjoying it. But you can't argue with him. Still, I really missed him now. And Brigid and the dogs. I actually longed to take them for a walk. Funny, it seemed the nicest, most ordinary thing in the world to walk the dogs before bed. I hadn't appreciated our life with Grandfather.

"If you ask me, the whole thing stinks," my sister said. "That Mrs Hanna's a crook!"

"I suppose Heather's a prisoner," I said. "In Piccadilly Circus."

That shut her up. She never liked to be reminded of her foolishness. Or her terribly headstrong character.

But something was definitely wrong. It's easy to say after the event what one should or should not have done. Maybe it was a case for the police? But I hated them. They might find out we had faked ID's. Maybe that was a crime. And look what had happened in Piccadilly? Sister Martin says fear of authority is in the Irish genes - from being oppressed so long. But what about the missing painting? The accusation might be true. By going to the police I might find out Heather was a thief. And this was the last thing I wanted to hear. She was always short of money. The last time she came to Dublin, she'd never let us into her hotel room.

My other dread was that she'd started drinking like Dad. Why did adults do it? There was no way I'd ever ruin my brain.

While I kept on being a Russian General and doing nothing, Katie kept up her nagging. "Hercule Poirot would advertise," she said one night in bed.

I stared into the dark. "In which paper?"

"He'd try them all."

"Hmm. He could pay for it."

I lay there thinking. It was true - they always advertised in books. But this was life. Had we become characters in some thriller? I remembered the film, *Desperately Seeking Susan*. In that they'd advertised a lot. So maybe we should? But what papers did Heather read? She used to read books mainly. She'd even sent me a novel by Henry James which Sister Martin said was too advanced for me, although it wasn't. But what did we know of our own mother's habits now? We'd seen very little of her over the last four years. She liked clothes and make-up, and read magazines rather than newspapers. *The Guardian* was left-wing, but she wasn't political. Maybe we should try *The Times*?

So with our first wages we put a small ad in its 'Miscellaneous' column: *Heather Kelly, please contact Clare at 071-221-1666.*

We told the receptionist to expect an important call.

We waited.

But days passed and none came.

Our money was completely wasted. So much for Katie's ideas.

Eleven

Time's meant to be an illusion, and it seemed so to us in those first weeks in London. We were going from day to day like people in a bad dream. Or people on a treadmill. What were we to do next? I didn't know. I couldn't think of anything. It was like the time I'd left Heather locked out all night. I didn't know then either. But then I was only twelve. Now I was sixteen. I knew she was in trouble. Yet I was doing nothing. Grandfather could call me "sensible", but it was no use to me now. Nothing in my experience compared with this. Or prepared me for it. Winning book prizes for lessons or green ribbons for good behaviour in school didn't qualify you for finding a mother. We were lulled into a trance of disappointed expectation. We began to realise Heather was lost. She hadn't just forgotten to come to Euston. Something was wrong. Either she had amnesia. Or else she was guilty.

Then something terrible happened. It was so awful, it put everything else out of our heads. I mean we even stopped thinking of Heather for a few days.

Sister Martin was always going on about the modern world being a "hissing cauldron of lust." It was a quotation from some saint's memoirs. I think she's wrong about that, Dublin's pretty tame. Nothing much happens there. But London was another matter. The hotel festered with sex. It permeated everything like a miasma. As I said, the night porter always teased us. And one of the kitchen porters propositioned me in a most vulgar way. He actually showed me his penis, asking what I thought of his "banana?" It was disgusting. I said I hated bananas. Later Katie and I burst out laughing - we knew the facts of life. Everyone in school did.

But one day we looked into the cauldron. We were coming downstairs with our brushes and mops etc, when we heard a scream.

It was from 129, the French professor's room.

We stopped outside.

"Bastard!" a woman's voice screamed.

It sounded like Mary Murphy.

"Oh, ye bastard. Get off me!"

I looked at Katie, wondering what to do. We'd got into such trouble before.

"Open it," she whispered.

"I can't."

We walked on.

"Please, someone help!"

I used my master key.

The professor had Mary pinioned on a bed. His trousers were down and he was trying to commit a rape on her.

I was frozen.

"Stop it! Stop it!" Katie yelled.

He turned round. His penis protruded over his trousers.

We gaped.

He pulled them up, yelling, "Get out! Get out!"

We stood our ground.

But he didn't attack us.

"Notheeng happen! Notheeng happen!" he yelled, tearing out of the door and down the corridor.

Mary was sitting on the bed, sobbing and shaking. Her long red hair was tossed and her stockings were torn. "Did you see that? Did you see what the fecker did?"

While Katie comforted her, I rang the porter.

The Frenchman was caught in the foyer.

The police came and arrested him. We were brought down to the police station in a squad car, tearing the wrong way down Oxford Street. It happened so quickly, we didn't have time to be nervous. A plainclothes woman officer questioned us separately, in a drab little room.

"I want you to describe exactly what you saw, Clare," she said kindly.

I did, saying how we went in when we heard Mary scream.

"Had he penetrated her?" the woman perused my face.

"I couldn't tell." I went red. It was stupid. She was a nice woman. "He jumped up and ran out."

She wrote everything down and asked me to sign it.

She was so nice, I thought of telling her about Heather. But I just couldn't get the words out. I was too afraid. And I'd instructed Katie not to mention it either. Maybe we should have. Those police seemed OK. But I couldn't. I mean, you could be nearly arrested for asking directions. And put in care for being under sixteen.

The Frenchman claimed Mary was willing, but she denied it. Finally he was let go because she wasn't actually raped. And anyhow she wouldn't sign the statement. She didn't want to press charges because her family in Ireland might find out and never speak to her again. It didn't make sense. I tried to tell her this, but she wouldn't listen.

"I'd never be able to face them," she sobbed.

"Don't be silly!" I said. "They'll understand. It was nothing to do with you."

But she wouldn't listen to me. What kind of people

were they? What if Grandfather had blamed us when our father had attacked us? It was the same thing. Well, not quite - our Dad wasn't like *that*. But you know what I mean.

I tried again. "Why don't you write down what happened. I'll bring it to the station."

"But I can't read or write!" And she broke into worse sobbing. "That's why I was afraid to sign."

I was shocked. Why hadn't she learned in school? I felt really, really sorry for Mary. We were only working for the summer, but she was probably condemned forever to a life of slavery. Some Irish politicians were inclined to say how good emigration was. How you should see the world - and that sort of thing. But had they ever cleaned out foreign toilets? That's the only sort of job a girl like Mary could get. I offered to help with her reading. And to help her write out what happened. But she wouldn't agree to press charges. Not with attempted rape even. She was too afraid of her family.

One thing: it cleared up the misunderstandings between us. All along, she had thought we were "Dubs." And that all Dubs were snobs. It was the same with school. Everyone thought Mount Prospect girls were snobs. But we weren't. Now Mary's accusation really shocked me. Were we? I told her we couldn't help coming from Dublin, anymore than she could help being from the country. Prejudice comes from not knowing people properly. And I don't think we're snobs. I hope not.

But although something good came from the ill-wind of Mary's experience, I worried about Katie. After all, she was hardly fifteen. What if it affected her later? Already she hated men because of our father. But she was tough enough and it seemed to run off her.

Although sorry for Mary, she was intrigued by the drama. Her Cruella de Vil theories about goodies and baddies were being justified. And the other people in the hotel were really nice. Even Jennifer was kind.

"I've poached you a couple of eggs, love," he said to Katie the morning after the attempted rape.

Katie reddened in embarassment. "Eh - thanks."

As she took them, he said, "What about you, Clare?"

"I'm a cereal person, thanks."

"You girls were heroines to stop that bastard." And he went away, muttering about the world going to pot.

So things settled down again. Mary was given two weeks' compassionate leave. And the Frenchman had left the hotel. Awful as he'd been, we soon forgot him. We had the worry of Heather.

It was obvious she was having another breakdown. I looked up some hospitals in the phone book. But there were so many, I didn't know where to even start enquiring.

Katie suggested hiring a detective. I poopood that too. It was too dramatic. And how were we to pay for it? But still we borrowed the Yellow Pages from the reception desk and checked under Detectives. If you think they just exist in stories, or on TV, well you're wrong. Look up the phone book. Just look, 'Enry 'Iggins. There were about four or five pages of private detectives advertised. Look, if you don't believe me. It's true.

Katie was reading out one of the ads. "*Archer Investigations*. He's Sam Spade's partner."

"Whose partner?"

"Sam Spade - he's a detective in a book Grandad lent me, *The Maltese Falcon*."

"I'm sure it's a different Archer," I said. We weren't in one of her damn books.

Then she read on, "*All private and commercial investigations undertaken. Surveillance, process serving. Missing persons traced* - let's ring him!"

"No!" The idea gave me the creeps. And God knows what it would cost.

I grabbed the phone book. There was one ad for an agency with a drawing of Sherlock Holmes.

For God's sake, detectives existed. An ad for Social Workers said they were specialists in tracing missing family members. But the very idea of them put me off. A social worker might ring our Grandfather. Or send us right back to Ireland. An ad for *A Beresford Clarke* looked smaller than the others;

Personal Services. Discreet and private investigations personal enquiries. Process serving and legal advice. Free advice/quotations. Lombard House, Lancaster Gate.

It was mental, but I was too nervous to ring up. Still we had to do something soon. We couldn't go on like this. Sister Martin had been angry with me once and called me a procrastinating character. Maybe she was right. Maybe I was. I went on and on in a dreamy way. But what if a detective called Heather a thief too? It was something I didn't want to hear.

I was getting more and more depressed. I even missed Grandfather and Brigid. Would he be able to manage the garden on his own? Maybe we should have taken his advice and stayed in Dublin. I began to wonder about his relationship with Heather. Was it possible that Heather had treated him the way she was treating us? Was Grandfather's attitude just a natural reaction to an impossible person? After all, Heather was his only child. And Grandfather's marriage hadn't been all that happy. He'd been let down by someone in his youth, a woman who wanted to marry someone rich. So he'd married another woman, our grandmother. She died but I remembered her vaguely. She was ancient and never spoke, only grunted at us to keep quiet. We were always being told not to make noise round her. To go out to the garden and play. She wasn't a happy person. Brigid told me that on their wedding morning, Granny's father had come to her and said, "Just say the word and I'll call this off." She just glared at him, saying, "How dare you speak to me like that!" It was really dramatic. There she was all dressed up and ready to go to the church. The marriage was never happy, though, according to Brigid. Still, I couldn't believe it was all Grandfather's fault. He was an oddity, but he had his good points. After all, he looked after Brigid and us. And he wasn't particularly rich, just careful. When Heather was born, Grandfather doted on her. But by the time she was our age, he was too strict. He'd never let her out on dates. Heather once told me he'd gone into the drawingroom when she was kissing Daddy and told him to go home. Then they fell out over the marriage. It was so sad. Instead of gaining a son, he'd gained a drunkard. And lost a daughter.

On our next half-day Katie said, "Let's go to Walton Street."

She was sitting on the floor doing sit-ups to lose weight from all the junk food she'd been eating. I was lying on my bed, too depressed to even read. My concentration had gone to pot. I'd read exactly two pages of my Sartre book. "What for?"

"It's the scene of the crime. We might get a lead."

I gave her a withering look. "Don't be stupid!"

Katie burst into tears.

I put an arm round her. Why couldn't I be a kind big

sister? Why was I always sarcastic? I took everything out on her. "Sorry!"

"You're always calling me stupid!"

"Sorry!" The strain was beginning to get to us. We were both desperately on edge.

After awhile Katie cheered up - she always forgave me. "What if the picture wasn't stolen. What if Mrs Hanna framed Heather?"

I sighed. "You're using very emotional language. And why should she?"

"*Cherchez la femme.*"

"Oh, Katie." But I didn't say shut up. I just thought how awkwardly cuddly she was.

It seemed harmless enough to walk past the house. So we took the Underground to Knightsbridge that afternoon. It was busy with shoppers. Tourists flocked out of Harrods. Everyone was so carefree. Why were we exceptions to the universe? We'd come to London to see Heather and have fun. So far neither had been achieved. We'd done nothing. Not even seen Buckingham Palace or the changing of the guard. Katie would never admit it but she was hoping for a glimpse of Princess Diana or Fergie coming out. Even Wally hadn't got in touch. I'd written to his home about our change of address, but received no reply. Walking down the Brompton Road, Katie admired herself in the shop windows - she has a habit of doing this. But I pretended not to notice. Then she saw a dress in a boutique. It was a leopard mini-dress and looked really punk on her. But she wanted it, so we bought it. I had to make up for making her cry - she's mad about clothes, and anyhow it was her birthday soon. Also she'd spent all her money on a Claddagh ring for my last birthday. Then we sauntered down Beauchamp Place and round to Walton Street. We were doing something, at least.

Number 26A showed no sign of life. The Georgian windows were blinded by thick white curtains, and the solid black door was closed like a fortress against us.

Katie leaned over the railings to touch the tree. "The basement window's open."

I pulled her on nervously. It was a public street and there was no reason why we couldn't walk there, but still I felt like a criminal. What if we were seen?

"The picture's probably in the house," Katie whispered. "Mrs Hanna must have hidden it."

"Surely she wouldn't risk that?" I played her game. "She'd hide it somewhere else."

At that stage I didn't really know what to believe. We walked to the end of the street and then back. As we passed the house again, the door suddenly opened and someone came out.

It was Mrs Hanna. I recognised her ox-like body. Her tuft of red hair and thick myopic glasses.

At first she didn't notice us. She just shut the door, and came down the steps, fumbling with her bag.

Then Katie had to nudge me. "She's wearing heely-highs."

The woman heard this and, looking up sharply, saw us. "What are you doing here?"

"It's a public street!" Katie cheeked her.

The woman sort of puffed out her cheeks. She looked as if she'd explode. Then came for us across the pavement, waving an umbrella. "Be off! Or I'll call the police!"

We fled to a Knightsbridge café.

Katie ordered her usual pizza.

I was trembling too much to eat. "You needn't have drawn attention to us!"

My sister took a huge bite, completely unaffected.

"She's a crook. Maybe we should house the search."

"Talk properly!"

She stuffed more food into her mouth. "Remember Heather had the weekends off?"

"Do you want to end up in jail?"

"Heather said he went to a country house."

I ignored her, looking out the café window to the street. I wasn't getting into a fight with her. If I said anything she might decide to act on her own. My sister's like that, as you'll remember from before. My best way of dealing with her was not to have a head-on conflict. I knew this from experience. After a while I registered something. The sweeper in the street looked awfully like Wally. His ponytail had been cut, but he was wearing his Trotskyite glasses. I perused the figure. It was him, OK. I know the coincidence will never be believed. But I can't help it. Anything can happen, 'Enry 'Iggins. I know that now. We saw him sweeping the street. It happened just like that. It really did.

I watched as he meticulously swept some papers into a pile, put them on a shovel and tossed them into his little red cart. Then I ran out. "Wally!"

He was suntanned and healthier-looking. Seeing me, he dropped his brush and hugged me. "Clare!"

It was a miracle. Maybe there was a God.

I was in tears.

"I called to the Cumberland, but no one had heard of you."

"Didn't they say we were in the Imperial?"

They hadn't.

Maybe it was the same with Heather.

I told him about her being missing. It all came out in a babble of incomprehension.

"Wait!" he said. "You mean she never came to

Euston?"

I nodded.

He shook his head in puzzlement. "That's strange."

He wasn't off duty for another hour, so we agreed to meet later in the same café. To use up the time, we looked around Harrods for an hour. It was the most beautiful shop I'd ever seen. The food shop went on for rooms and rooms and rooms. I'd never seen so many different brands of ham and duck and stuff. It certainly cut Brown Thomas's in Dublin down to size. I'll never be intimidated by them again.

Then we went back to the café and Wally came back, looking as if he'd had a shower. His jeans were stiff and new and all wrong with his Donegal tweed jacket.

"Why haven't you been to the police?" was the first thing he said.

Then it all came out about the picture. I thought he'd think badly of Heather. But he just slurped his coffee noisily. "Hmm. That woman acted very oddly. Why'd she chase you away?"

"She's guilty," Katie said, her chin in her hands.

"It looks like it," Wally said.

I could've hugged him.

Then he studied Heather's letter inviting us. "There must be an explanation."

I looked at him wearily. "We keep thinking she'll turn up, but she doesn't. Katie wants to hire a detective."

"Well, that's not a bad idea."

But I still resisted. Surely it'd cost a lot? More than we had? We'd already wasted money on that ad. But meeting Wally lifted our spirits. He was a friend from a happier time. I think I loved him now. I certainly appreciated him more. Again, I felt my feelings in a new way. Why does it take a crisis? Now I missed

Grandfather because we were in trouble. And did I just miss Heather because we never saw her? It was such a relief to tell someone. We sat in that café, talking till we were tired out like old times. Then he saw us back to the hotel, saying he'd be in touch.

Twelve

Now I was fired up to do something. Maybe ring a detective at last. I'd just dial the number. If it didn't work out, I could hang up. Whatever we found out, whatever the detective said, couldn't be as bad as this inertia. This endless not knowing.

But before I could, Miss King gave me a letter. "This is for you, Kelly."

Was it from Heather? Maybe she'd seen our ad?

I examined it, my hand shaking. But it wasn't her writing. The envelope was addressed to Miss Clare Kelly, in anonymous hand printed capitals.

"Open it!" Katie said.

I did. Inside someone had printed in bits of newspaper: AS YOU VALUE YOUR LIFE AND REASON, STAY AWAY FROM LONDON.

Katie grabbed it. "It's from Heather!"

I shook my head in disbelief. "No."

"But it's in code! She's trying to warn us!"

"Why didn't she just write?"

But Katie was jumping up and down with

excitement. "It's nearly the same message as Sherlock Holmes got in *The Hound of the Baskervilles!*"

"Oh, give over!" Sometimes my sister was too much. Despite all that happened, it was outlandish to think Heather would resort to such disguises. Why should she?

"But Heather sent me that book for Christmas. She knows I'll recognise the quote."

I didn't answer. I was losing patience.

My sister was mental. But that very afternoon she dragged me to a bookshop. We found a copy of Conan Doyle's stories. She was right: Sherlock Holmes did get a message like ours. Except he was told to stay away from the "moor." I felt like pinching myself. Life had turned into a nightmare. Except we were awake. All Katie's fantasies had become reality. On top of a missing mother, the picture accusation, Jennifer and the attempted rape, this was absolutely weird. But it happened, 'Enry 'Iggins. It did.

Heather was daft, but not that daft.

I was the "sensible" one. I had to keep my head, but it was difficult. Things were really going crazy now. We had fallen, like Alice, into a mad upside down world. Into a hissing cauldron full of strange inhabitants. And even stranger things were to happen before we found Heather.

About two days later the Spanish Housekeeper called me to the phone, with a little lecture about personal calls being forbidden during worktime.

"I'm sorry," I mumbled, my heart stopping.

I knew it wasn't Wally. It wasn't Grandfather either. He wasn't a phoner. It must be Heather. It had to be. She had found us at last. Probably through the Cumberland. What a good thing I'd left our address with them. All the way downstairs, I rehearsed what

Has Anyone Seen Heather?

I'd say. You're our mother. How could you treat us like this? Why didn't you come to Euston? At first I'd be cross, but then I'd relent and forgive her. I'd have to forgive her. You couldn't stay angry with Heather.

The receptionist directed me to a phone booth in the lobby.

"Hello," I said worriedly. "Heather?"

Someone was breathing heavily on the other end.

"Is that you, Heather?"

More breathing.

"Hello, Heather?"

Silence.

"Get out of London," a voice said - it sounded female or a man pretending.

That evening, I phoned Wally. He came over immediately. He stared at our strange note as we walked down the Bayswater Road. "I wish you'd go to the police, Clare," he said in his high voice.

"They'll only send us home."

He stopped me, staring into my face. "But why?"

"Katie's under sixteen. They might find out."

"Oh, I forgot that." He let me go and we walked on. "But that phone call was sinister. What if the person gets violent?"

I shrugged. "It could be a joke."

No matter what he said, I wouldn't go to the police. How could I? I was too afraid of them. Besides, it might draw attention to Heather. What if she was hiding out? What if they found her and brought her to prison?

"Well, hire a detective then," he nagged.

But I was still afraid to ring one. I told myself it might cost more than we had. Fear had immobilised me, I knew. When we still wouldn't do anything, Wally begged us to change jobs at least. He kept nagging that someone wanted us out of London. And that someone might harm us.

So I bought the paper and looked up jobs, but without luck. I kept telling myself the caller could be a practical joker. And the letter must be from the same person. They could've been sent by the other Irish staff. But, since we had saved Mary, they continued being nicer to us. Although Jennifer was often odd. After all, my only definite impression of the voice on the phone was that it was a man pretending to be a woman. Maybe it was him? I decided to ask him outright.

On one half-day he came into the kitchen when we were having lunch. He was all dressed up in his ladies' clothes. He looked OK, except for his legs which were too skinny, sort of muscular.

Seeing us, he said, "That's a nice dress Katie."

Katie was wearing her new leopard mini. "Thanks."

"Clare, you should do more with yourself."

I shrugged. "I'm not interested in clothes."

Katie said petulantly. "She won't let me buy anything."

I glared. It wasn't true. What about her leopard dress?

"How are you going to get a husband?"

I shrugged again. That was really low on my list.

He wiggled over behind the grill. Took off his wig and put on his chef's uniform of a white coat and apron and hat. "You should use make-up, Clare. And show off your legs like Katie."

I said nothing.

"Come on, ducks. Tell Aunt Jennifer what's wrong."

I showed him our hate note.

He scanned it. "Someone's playing a joke on you."

"We got a phone call too," I stared meaningfully at him.

He didn't react. He just shrugged, saying, "Sticks and stones will break my bones, but names will never hurt me."

It couldn't be him.

"You know why all this is happening, don't you? Venus is in retrograde. And the moon is waning. When that happens, nothing can go right."

I said nothing. After all, astrology was no worse than believing in angels. Jennifer was mental, but nice. I've never met a mental person who wasn't really, really nice - even Brigid. And maybe Jennifer wasn't so mad. Maybe the world would be saner if men wore women's clothes and we wore men's. Maybe it'd even things out. The next day he gave each of us a lipstick. But they were too red to use. His/her kindness was an indication of our new popularity. Now everyone liked us. No, the phone call couldn't be from anyone at the hotel.

"It's Mrs Hanna," Katie kept insisting.

I sighed. "What's Hecuba to him, or he to Hecuba."

"What do you mean?"

"Read *Hamlet*."

She turned to the wall. "You're always talking rot!"

Since coming to London, I thought that play was written for me. I now understood the melancholy Dane. I had the same inertia. To do or not to do, that was the problem. While Katie slept, I tossed and turned and tormented myself. "Get out of London," the voice kept saying in my head. It was so sinister. It had sounded female. It could be Mrs Hanna. After all she'd chased us down the street. And could trace us through the Cumberland. It was the stuff of fiction. Then so was Heather's disappearance. So was everything since we arrived in this crazy place. That night I had my dream again. This time Daddy was helping us look for her. He was dressed in an evening suit and wore a hat like Fred Astaire. Except his eyes were red-rimmed from crying. It's funny we always just accepted his leaving. We never tried to find him. He was somewhere in England. But never wrote. I always thought he was having another affair. But maybe he was sorry? He sent us kilts one Christmas - a red one for Katie and a green one for me. They were too frumpy to wear but maybe he loved us. After all, he'd nearly broken down Grandfather's door. "Give me back my children!" was etched forever into my soul. Maybe he wouldn't have hit us again. Maybe he just wanted us back. In a way, I loved him. He was our father, after all.

I studied the Situations Vacant. There was nothing suitable, live-in. Wally was still afraid whoever was threatening us would do something really violent. So he kept nagging me to go to the police. I was still dead set against them. So when Katie borrowed the Yellow Pages from reception again, I rang A Beresford Clarke, Private Investigator, for an appointment. After all, he'd advertised "free advice."

I didn't know what to expect. Katie told me she imagined someone like Sherlock Holmes. My idea was someone kind, like the Equalizer or John Morse, maybe with a fedora hat. Ours couldn't have been more different. He had a seedy office on the top floor of a big house near Lancaster Gate. Everything about him was untidy.

When we rang his bell, a voice yelled through the intercom, "Push the door!"

We did, but it wouldn't open.

So we rang again.

"Push the door!" the same voice screamed.

This time we got in. Then we headed up three flights of rickety stairs to his office door.

Our knock brought the same exasperated shout, "Come in!"

A Beresford-Clarke sat behind a big desk littered with papers. There was torn lino on the floor, a couch with the stuffing coming out in one corner. He was talking on the phone and pointed us to a couple of wobbly chairs. He was nearly bald, about thirty-five and pudgy, with a drinker's pink face. And small blue eyes which watched us warily as we waited. Really, he looked like a race-course type. A bookie or something. Or someone who'd hang round a pub.

Finally he put down the receiver and reached boredly for an appointment book. "Let's see - which of you is Miss Kelly?"

"I'm Ms Kelly and this is my sister Katie."

"We want you to find someone," she said.

He winced, as if in pain.

I gave my sister a silencing look. "Eh - how much do you cost?"

"About twenty pounds an hour."

"We'll hire you for half-an-hour," Katie said.

He looked at her in amazement

I glared at her to shut up, then said, "You said something about a free consultation."

He grimaced. "That means I won't charge to tell you if I can help you."

"Oh, well - we've lost our mother."

"And now someone's threatening us," Katie butted in. "There may be a connection."

He held up his hand like a traffic policeman. "Just a minute. You've lost your mother and someone's threatening you?"

I reached into my bag. "Yes. We got this in the post."

He read it, laughing shortly. Then he dropped it onto the desk, looking us over warily.

Has Anyone Seen Heather?

"We got a funny phone call after that," I said.

He raised his eyebrows. "Why funny?"

"We were told to get out of London," Katie added.

He pushed back his chair. "I'm afraid, I don't act for children."

"I'm eighteen," I lied.

He just smiled. "Are you now?"

Of course, I went crimson. I was always telling stupid lies. But no one so far in London had questioned our age. And the students in the hostel had thought we were old enough to go into a pub.

He cupped his hands behind his head and leaned back in his chair, looking at us cynically. "I might be too expensive for you."

"We'll give you a trial," Katie snapped.

He let out a short laugh.

"We can get money," I said. "We both have jobs."

He looked dubiously from one to the other. "Where do you work?"

"We're chamberpersons in the Imperial Hotel."

He laughed again.

"Oh, don't worry about your fee!" Katie snapped.

He wagged a finger warningly. "I don't act for children!"

She went on obstinately. "You shouldn't discriminate against us. It's ageism!"

He and Katie had a definite personality clash. I thought he'd throw us out. But instead, he yawned lazily. Then he cupped his head again and leaned back in his swivel chair. "Why do you think your mother's missing?"

I showed him her letter. "She didn't meet us."

He studied it. "You wired her?"

I nodded.

"She may not have got the wire." He gave me back

the letter. "Funny, it's usually parents who are looking for their delinquent children."

Katie reddened. "We're not delinquents!"

"Another word and you go outside!" he snapped. Then to me, "You normally live with your grandmother?"

"Grandfather. In Dublin."

"Do you have a father?"

"No - he left us."

A Beresford Clarke sighed heavily. "To lose one parent is a misfortune, but to lose two is downright careless!"

It was a cliché from Oscar Wilde. I remembered my father had once acted in that play. He was Algernon. But it was tasteless of the detective to say that. It wasn't funny. And it set my sister off again. "It wasn't our fault!"

He got up and opened the door. "Would you mind waiting outside?"

She obeyed, her face blotchy with anger.

"Look," I said, "she's upset."

He held up the note, whispering, "Are you sure she didn't write this?"

I shook my head. "No, she wouldn't."

He snorted in disbelief. "I'm not so sure. She obviously enjoys drama."

"She didn't."

He rubbed his pudgy cheeks. "How long have you lived with your grandmother."

"Grandfather. About four years."

"So he's your guardian. Arranged by your mother?"

I nodded. "Sort of." I couldn't go into the fight with Dad.

He snapped his diary shut. "Because your mother didn't turn up doesn't mean she's missing."

"But she wrote."

He pushed back his chair. "Well, she obviously changed her mind."

"But she wouldn't."

He smirked, nodding towards the door. "Hmm ... You're both so charming?"

He certainly didn't like us.

He stood up and went to the window. "She might have written again, changing plans. You can never count on a letter arriving. But tell me one thing."

I looked up. "What?"

"If you're so worried, why didn't you go to the police?"

"Because her employer accused her of taking a picture," I heard myself say. "A Turner."

He let out a whistle. "Well, then I'd say she's definitely not in a position to entertain children! Why didn't you tell me?"

I hated him. "I thought it wasn't important."

"It's important, all right. But I can't act for someone who can't tell the truth."

I was dying with embarrassment. "I've told you everything now."

He laughed, saying in a gravelly American accent. "Do you take me for a sap? Your sister writes herself a hate letter. Now you tell me your mother's an art thief!"

Sweat dripped down my armpits. I felt faint. "My sister didn't write the letter! And my mother's not a thief!"

He leaned over the desk. "Well then, it's a joke. Someone at the hotel. Why don't you go back to Dublin? Your mother'll turn up there."

I groped awkwardly in my bag. "I'll pay you anything."

He waved his hand. "You can put away the dough!"

Then he went over to a filing cabinet and pulled out a drawer. "See those!" He ran pudgy fingers over fat grubby files. "All missing persons. Some of them went out for cigarettes and were never heard from again."

I caught my breath. Would we ever see Heather again?

His blue eyes were surrounded by millions of tiny wrinkles. Now they bored into me. "At any one time there are about 400,000 people in Britain no longer known at their old address. Over 150,000 of these are actually missing. But cheer up - most of them return within a week!"

"Heather's gone longer than a week."

"She's hiding - that's all." And he showed me to the door. "I'm afraid there's nothing I can do."

So much for our detective. It was just like I thought it'd be. He didn't think Heather was missing. He just thought she was a thief and didn't even believe us about the letter and phone call. Looking back, I don't blame him. Trouble usually comes in threes, but who'd believe our string of misfortunes? I mean, everything was so cracked. Sister Martin says God sends you the grace for life's difficult moments. This was our time of trial. I didn't believe in a personal God. But someone was giving us the strength. Maybe it was true about angels. Although the detective advised us to go home, we were determined to stay. And the Imperial might be a dead end. But it was also the only means to an end - finding Heather.

Thirteen

In the middle of our third week in London, I saw an in the *Evening Standard*:

WANTED
Two attractive barmaids for Thameside Inn. Live-in. Good Pay and conditions for experienced applicants. Apply: The Manager, William Shakespeare's Inn. Bankside, London SW Tel: 071-407-7777.

I'd no pub experience and Katie'd never been in one. And as for being attractive ... well, Katie's beautiful, but they'd want someone older. Still the name, William Shakespeare, drew me. I rang and was given an interview that afternoon. It was a waste of money for us both to go. And Katie's age might put them off. So she turned down the beds alone, while I took the Circle Line to Monument.

It was my first journey without her. At first, it was OK. I read the ads: MAKE EVERY DAY A RED LITTER DAY and THE END OF THE LINE FOR LITTER. But then my imagination began to run amok. In the airless caverns of the Underground, I kept getting crazy thoughts. Was Heather dead? Who'd sent the note? Was the phone call from the same person? Who? And was that someone watching us? Maybe following me now?

A train screeched up and the crowd piled in.

I sat opposite a foreign-looking man with a sinister moustache.

He'd been on the platform. Now he was staring.

Our eyes met.

Was he following me?

To calm myself, I studied the ads in the train. Some of them were for temps. If only I could type. Or do word-processing. Then we wouldn't have to slave like scullions. We'd have money for clothes - like all the other girls you saw in London. Katie wanted them, but I only wanted household stuff for our flat with Heather.

The train stopped and the man got out.

I was getting paranoid.

The girl in the ad was brimming with Poise and Personality. We'd had lectures on that in school. Also typing was offered last year. But I'd done extra English instead. Grandfather said I'd live to regret it. He was right. He was always right.

William Shakespeare's Inn was by the Thames all right, in sight of Southwark Bridge and beside the railway bridge for Cannon Street Station. To get to it, you crossed Southwark Bridge, then went down narrow steps to Bankside. It had a deck over the river. Inside, quaint Tudor-style rooms led into each other, while little staircases led up to the restaurant. It was an old pub in every sense. I mean, the carpet was worn, but the overhead wooden beams were stained attractively. The staff wore Elizabethan clothes - orange and green dirndl skirts and bodices for the women and green waistcoats and trousers for the men.

The manager was a well-dressed cockney type with dark slicked-down hair and hooded eyelids. His name was Mr Williams. When I told him about Katie, the first thing he quizzed me about was age.

"Is everyone over eighteen?"

I said I was, but Katie wasn't quite. I was afraid to tell a complete lie.

"Hmm ... She'll have to stay in the restaurant, then,"

he said, leaning against the bar. "We normally only employ staff over eighteen. But ..." he eyed me sort of flirtatiously. "I can make an exception since it's only for the summer. Enjoying London?"

"Yes," I lied, smiling. I knew what was expected of me. Just as we had to be obedient schoolgirls with Miss King, I had to flirt with Mr Williams. He was sexist, but nice.

"When can you start?" he asked.

We seemed to have the jobs. "Would Friday be OK?"

Thursday was payday at the Imperial. I had to be sure of our money.

He calculated mentally. "This is Monday. That's fine. Coffee?"

I nodded and he called to the barmaid. "Bring us two coffees, Liz." She was a very buxom blonde Northerner, I later got to know and like.

As we drank, he talked nonstop about his holiday in Ireland.

It was a change that someone liked us.

"We took a jaunting car to Kate Kearney's Cottage. What a country. What are those wild red hedges?"

"Holly?"

"It was summer!"

"Fuschia?"

"That's it!"

Although I hated gardening, I knew something about plants, thanks to Grandfather.

Then he showed me through different bars with names like Anne Hathaway's Ale Bar, and the Globe. I was to work in the Ale bar. The house, he told me, had been visited by Dr Johnson in his day.

"I think he wrote plays too," Mr Williams said vaguely.

"No, it was a dictionary."

Has Anyone Seen Heather?

The famous letter to Lord Chesterfield was in our prose anthology. Sister Martin had told us about the dictionary. We Irish were much better educated than the English. All they talked about was sex and football.

"You'll be a super guide, Jane," Mr Williams said, shaking hands goodbye.

"Clare," I said.

"Clare! Of course!"

Maybe our luck was changing. Getting the jobs was the first good thing that happened. Back on Southwark Bridge, I looked down into the river trying to remember a line Wally was always quoting about the river being a strong brown god ... strong brown god. We needed some sort of a god.

William Shakespeare's turned up just in time. Because when I got back to the Imperial, Katie handed me a parcel. "This came in the post."

I handled it gingerly. "What is it?"

"Chocolates. They're poisoned."

"Ah, come on." I examined them. But they certainly weren't normal sweets, like say Cadburys. They were packed in a battered heart-shaped box with a vulgar rose on the lid. There were six sweets, whitish on the outside. One of them oozed stuff.

"They look stale." I picked one up.

"Don't touch them!"

After our hate letter and the phone call, I'd believe anything. Anything, 'Enry 'Iggins. We were in some crazy world where crazy rules applied. Although I poopooed Katie, I handled the box with great care, hiding it under our bed. Was someone trying to murder us now? If so it was another case for the police. But my fear of them remained. It would only come out about Heather, and I had to warn her first. And the detective wouldn't believe us either. After all, he didn't

Has Anyone Seen Heather?

believe us about the letter or the phone call. Everything was so crazy. We didn't know what to do, so again did nothing. Even Wally said on the phone, "Clare, are you imagining things?" He doubted us too. This was too much, even for him. And could you blame him? Still, it seemed to pacify him that we were leaving the hotel.

Our problem now was telling them we were leaving. It was mental, but I was afraid of Miss King. Although a feminist, I couldn't assert myself - it was just like leaving the cinema in Dublin. While we had inferiority complexes, Miss King was the opposite. She ruled by intimidation. After all, her country had ruled our country and a quarter of the globe. If they were all bullies like her, it was no wonder. We'd promised to stay till September and now were leaving without notice. She'd probably insult the Irish. Or keep our cards.

I wanted to flit. Just disappear without telling anyone. But then we wouldn't get our money. So I thought of a plan: That weekend, Miss King's place would be taken by Miss Lopez, her Spanish assistant. From school, I knew the Spaniards were terrible snobs. They'd never allow their daughters to work as maids. So I rang Wally asking for his help. Would he pretend he was our cousin sent by an angry father to bring us home?

He was puzzled. "But why's he so angry?"

"Cos we're working as maids."

"Why can't you just leave?"

I lowered my voice. "They might stop us."

He sighed. "It sounds melodramatic. Things are getting to you, Clare."

"What do you mean?"

"Your mother and that. It's making you paranoid."

He thought we were cracked, I knew. And maybe we

were. Still, he agreed to act the part of cousin and came on Friday afternoon to collect us.

When I was summoned to the foyer, he was waiting on a sofa. His new clothes were too big and ruined any impression of ferocity. He just looked lost.

He stood up dutifully, asking in his squeaky way, "Who'm I to see, Clare?"

I asked for Miss Lopez. Then nervously introduced my "cousin" come to take us home.

She looked doubtfully at Wally. "You are a cuzeen?"

Irately he waved a letter. "Yes! I've been sent by their father! They must come home at once!"

Her English wasn't good enough to argue.

She turned to me. "Do you weesh this, Clare?'

I shrugged helplessly. "We've no choice. I'm afraid our father is very strict."

She frowned. "But, what am I saying, you can stay here."

"But we have to go. He's fond of us, you see."

She agreed to get us our cards. And money.

Then Katie wobbled downstairs with our stuff and Wally escorted us out. It was so easy. Maybe we should've just left. Why tell lies when the truth is better? And there was no bigger lie than that our father was fond of us.

Fourteen

I sent Grandfather postcards regularly. The latest one read:

> *Having a super time. Have moved to a better job. Address above. We are near St Paul's and the site of the Globe. Heather sends love. See you soon. Lots of love, to you and Brigid from, Clare and Katie.*

William Shakespeare's really was a change in our luck. It was a definite oasis in that summer of discontent. Firstly, it was more money - over a hundred pounds a week and you could earn more with overtime. Also the people were nicer. Oh, we had to wear that capitalistic serving wench's outfit. But there was a happy atmosphere and we lived *en famille* with the other staff in a nearby house. On Sundays we were given lunch by the manager's wife, a smart Londoner. It was always the same and always delicious: roast lamb and a marrow dish cooked with wine and tomatoes à la garlic.

Katie worked in the restaurant because of her age and I was in charge of Anne Hathaway's public ale bar. It was a great responsibility. But once I got used to the different drinks, it wasn't hard. There were whiskeys, bitters, and shandies for the locals; gin and tonics, gin and its, and gin fizzes for the stockbrokers and lawyers who crowded in for lunch. That was the busiest time of day. For two hours, it was hectic. The same for Katie in the restaurant. Then things eased off and the pub shut for the afternoon. We'd go for a walk then. Or else for a rest before going back. In the evenings, locals came into the bar for a chat. And in fine weather, younger people loitered on the deck till dark. With the riverboats and sailing in the background, they looked like figures in an Impressionist painting.

We'd have been happy, except for Heather.

Katie wanted to advertise again. But I still hoped for something to happen. Heather'd surely turn up, I kept persuading myself. She was getting settled into a new job. Maybe we'd imagined everything that happened. We'd kept the chocolates under our bed, but perhaps they were OK. We were just paranoid, from being in a strange environment. I told myself all sorts of things. That things would turn out all right. That we were in some sort of frozen dream. Now at least we had more money. But we didn't know what to do with it. So we put another ad in *The Times*: HEATHER, RING CLARE AT 071-407-7777.

Not very original.

And there was no answer.

I rang Dublin again, asking if any letters had come. If Heather had phoned, it'd come out in conversation. This time Grandfather picked up the phone.

"Whom were you expecting to write, Clare?" he asked stiffly.

I kept my voice casual. "Oh, no one special. My report might come."

"But that's not due till August."

"That's right. I forgot."

Grandfather sighed. "Sometimes you're conveniently vague, Clare. How's Katie?"

"She's fine. Here she is." I passed the receiver.

What did he mean by me being conveniently vague? Did he suspect something? But Katie chatted cheerfully for a few minutes, seeming to banish Grandfather's suspicions. Then I said a cheerful goodbye.

"It's good of you to phone, Clare." Grandfather was trying to be nice.

I felt rotten.

"How's your mother?"

"Eh - she's fine, Grandad."

"You can give her my regards."

"I will."

Click. He hung up.

But at least he'd asked for Heather. Normally he wouldn't do this. Did it mean he was prepared to bury the hatchet at last? I loved Grandfather and hated deceiving him. I worried again about him managing the garden by himself over the summer. Lately it was getting too much for him. And now we were lying to him. But what else could we do? One whiff of something wrong and he'd be over to claim us. He'd be horrified to hear about the painting, and it'd confirm all his worst theories about Heather's irresponsibility. No, we had to protect her from Grandfather finding out. Otherwise it'd be another decade before she was forgiven for that. Oh, if only Heather would get in touch. If only we could think of something else to do to find her. But what? At least we were safer at the Inn. Mrs Hanna didn't know where we were now. And ironically we didn't get any more phone calls or letters. So perhaps she was the culprit. We tried to concentrate on our work.

By degrees we got friendly with Liz, the other barmaid. She was the pretty blonde girl who'd given me coffee at my interview. She was full of fun and jokes. While we hardly filled our laced Elizabethan blouses, she spilled out of hers. Instead of being embarassed, she flaunted it. Like all the English, she was obsessed from the waist down. Except she was nicer than most of them. There was something so gentle about her. But Jerry, her boyfriend, was the opposite. He was a red-faced, rough-looking older man of about thirty-two who wore shiny gangsterish suits with narrow legs and smoked cigarettes out of the side of his mouth. And he greased his hair like Elvis Presley. It was yukky. Sometimes he waited for Liz in the bar till closing-time. Then they went out and didn't come home till five or six in the morning. Once I heard screams and slaps in the night. And the next morning she laughed off a black eye and bruises on her arm.

I'd seen such marks before - on Heather. I knew the kind of man he was. I thought of complaining him to Mr Wiliams, but decided to wait and see if it happened again.

One night Liz came into our room. She was getting ready for a date. Her hair was still wet and she wore a black leather mini.

She wiggled her bottom. "What do ya think o' me gear?"

You could see her pants, but we both admired it.

"Do ya want to come for a drink with Jerry?"

I said no.

"How about you, luv?" she asked Katie.

"She can't," I said. "She doesn't drink." It was bad enough that she smoked. And since coming to London she did so openly.

Now she gave me a rebellious look. "Can't I go?"

I shook my head no.

"But you never go out!" Liz coaxed. "It'll be gas. Jerry's paying."

I resisted. I didn't like Jerry. He was a chauvinist. "We're not really in the mood, thanks."

"You worry too much!" Liz pirouetted in front of our mirror. "Your Mum's OK."

In a weak moment, I'd told her about Heather - you

know the way you give confidences.

"She's found a fella!" Liz went on preening herself.

I cleared my throat, saying slowly. "You mean a boyfriend?"

"Yeh! She's sold the picture and done a bunk to Spain."

"She's a bit old for boyfriends." I looked at Katie, who seemed shocked by the idea.

Liz giggled sexily. "Don't be so green! You're never too old! She's having a bit."

I suppose we were green, but it hadn't occurred to us.

I assured Katie it wasn't true. But Heather was still youngish. Maybe Liz was right. Hamlet's mother had married again. The heyday of the blood was never tame. After all, she'd left us once before. Walked out and left us to cope with Dad. And she didn't bother to make up with Grandfather. They never corresponded. I couldn't understand their vendetta. Once I asked Brigid was Heather adopted? But she assured me no. They were father and daughter and simply couldn't stand each other. How had it happened? Would it be the same with our father? He never wrote either. For all he cared, we could be dead.

One day in the Bar Liz said her period was late.

"You need an iron tonic," I said, pulling a pint. Grandfather recommended this to everyone.

She gave me a puzzled look. "Would that get rid of it?"

I looked at her closely. She didn't look anaemic. "Let me see the whites of your eyes."

"Pregnancy's got nothing to do with eyes!" Furiously she wiped the counter-top. "You've heard of it, haven't you?"

"Yes!" I was shocked, but tried to hide it. "Is Jerry the

father?"

She shrugged, her breasts popping up nerve-rackingly. "Dunno."

"Mr Williams?" I'd seen them joking.

This threw her into a fit of giggles. "I've never met such greenhorns!"

I was embarassed. "What do you mean?"

"He's gay!"

"But he's married!"

She kept on giggling, then finally got her breath. "On Saturday night they both go out with fellas!"

You could be sure of nothing. Why did people complicate their lives? Who had got Liz into trouble? I perused all the men who might qualify. The bar manager? The Italian chef? The sissyish university student cellarman? Whoever it was, she was having an abortion. There was no persuading her otherwise.

Katie was shocked. "She could let us adopt it."

"What'd we do with a baby?"

My sister sighed. "We could give it to Grandfather. He likes babies."

In school we'd had a lecture against abortion. SPUC, the 'pro lifers', had come and shown slides of aborted foetuses. It was horrible. One girl got sick. And someone else fainted. It was so awful, it put me off abortion. Although I might need one some day. You never know, but I hope not. Anyway, there was no stopping Liz. Maybe she was right? What was the point of having children? If she treated her children the way Heather treated us, it was better to abort. Why had Heather had us? Had we been mistakes, to be regretted the way she had regretted marrying Dad? Yet they'd been in love. I remembered them going out to parties a lot, after opening nights. In the good old days when Daddy was working. They'd come home and cook us breakfast. And we'd all sit around the table eating pancakes and golden syrup, which according to my father is a poor substitute for maple syrup. Those were the days we didn't go to school.

And Heather always took our side. She must love us. Once I was in trouble for Irish. We were in the Holy Faith in Glasnevin at the time. I had to change schools a lot then, because we moved house all the time. They were sadistic nuns, who had a strap in the office to hit you with. (It was before they changed the law; now you can't hit school children in Ireland.) I was sent to the office once, but went home instead. Heather didn't make me go back. Any normal mother would, but she let me leave the school.

No, I was sure she wanted us.

It was different for Liz. What would she do with a baby? How could she support one? Or who would look after it while she worked? That week, I collected her in a taxi from the clinic. It seemed a non-event to her. But she chatted so merrily, I knew she was upset. Men were awful. I'd never have spoken to Jerry again. But she went out with him that very night. It takes all sorts.

Otherwise life was normal, as normal as it could be without Heather. No one threatened us now. The people who came into the pub commented on our accents, but they were nicer than the hotel. I told one man I was Finnish and was believed. I'd denied my country, I know. But patriotism was alien to me. I couldn't stand all that Irish dancing stuff. And what did one country mean in the vastness of space? Why couldn't everyone be Earthians instead of French, or Irish, or Spanish? I mean, Earth is only one of so many planets. There's Venus and Mars and Uranus and Neptune, etc. If an asteroid hit us and vaporised the oceans, all life on earth would die. Or what if they heated up and flooded the land? It didn't bear thinking about. Or there could be tidal waves. Or the ozone layer could disappear any day now. Then patriotism would be obsolete.

In our time off, Katie and I went for walks. The area reeked with history. Nearby was Clink Street, the site of the famous prison. It led past the Southwark Cathedral ruin to where Shakespeare's Globe Theatre had been. They were digging up the site during the summer and the archaeologists often dropped into the pub. I loved to imagine the Bard had passed this way. Maybe he'd thought up some of the plays walking these very streets. There was a fruit market which reminded me of Dublin's Moore Street. In the distance were London Bridge and Tower Bridge. And there was always the Thames, that strong brown god rushing on to the Barrier and the Isle of Dogs. I told Katie stories about the riverside pirates, press gangs and smugglers who populated the place long ago. About the kings and queens whose barges had passed this way. We longed to take a cruise, but wouldn't spend the money. One day we walked down to the Tower of London but didn't go in. We had to save our money. We'd need it for Heather. And for furniture for the flat.

We were like puppets, waiting to be jiggled to life. Or butterflies in some sort of chrysalis. Wally showed up from time to time. One night he met us for the pictures in Leicester Square. It was *The Accidental Tourist* with William Hurt, which made me lonely for my Dad. Why had he never written? What sort of a father was he? Were all men like him? Look at how Grandfather treated Heather. Maybe if he'd been kinder, she wouldn't have come to England in the first place. Sitting in a café afterwards, while Katie wolfed down a pizza and chattered about the film, I pondered on the unfairness of life. Was it some sort of lottery? If there was a God, he certainly wasn't very active. On top of that he was male. And men had messed up the world with their wars and their coldness.

"Here," I passed Wally a tenner across the table when time came to pay. After that first day, I never trusted Katie with money.

"It's my treat, Clare," he insisted.

Sometimes Wally gets on my nerves. Now he was trying to impress Katie.

"I'd prefer to go Dutch."

He folded his arms. "I'm not taking it."

"You're being sexist."

"Clare," he peered patronizingly over his glasses.

"You're always saying people shouldn't be dependent!" I snapped angrily. "Now you're acting like the rest of your sex."

He raised one eyebrow, paling. "How come?"

"You're messing up the world!"

He reddened. "Clare, you'll have to learn to be gracious! It's Katie's birthday." Lately he was coming the heavy. Which didn't suit him. He was too skinny.

"Then pay for her! I have my principles!"

"She's very high and mighty," Katie quipped.

Well, that was loyalty. I wanted to kill her, but instead burst into tears.

Katie groaned. "There's no need to over-react!"

"It's better than over-eating!" I gave her a dirty look.

Katie was furious. "I don't over-eat!"

"You do! You gobble everything like a pig!"

Next thing she was in tears. Why was I so mean?

Wally was now looking nervously round. "Clare, what's up? Pay if you like."

But I couldn't stop crying. The two of us sat there,

bawling.

He turned agitatedly to Katie. "Now, stop this."

I dried my eyes. "I can't stand it anymore. We'll never find Heather!"

Of course, I'd been desperately mean. I'd hurt Katie and Wally. He wasn't a chauvinist. He was only trying to be nice. In the end he got his way and paid. Would I ever be able to cope?

Fifteen

One morning Mr Williams handed me a letter. It was Heather's writing.

I tore it open.

Darlings,
Forgive this haste. Sorry all plans cancelled will be in touch. Things hectic here. Writing,
Love Heather.

Katie and I stared at it - at last we'd heard from her. Grandfather had sent it on.

I examined the stamp mark. It was marked June 16th, the day before we left Dublin. There were all sorts of scribbles on the envelope. "Try Ludlow," "Blackpool" and "Not known here."

Heather had addressed it to Grandfather's but had forgotten to put Dublin or Ireland.

So it'd been all over.

"See, there's a normal explanation," I said.

"But where is she now?" Katie said.

It was a good question.

"There's still Mrs Hanna. And the note! And the phone call, and those chocolates!"

Katie's imagination was running wild again. She was still sure we were in some sort of conspiracy. Despite all that had happened, I now put aside any theories about Heather being in danger. The letter sounded so normal. We'd get another one soon. It'd have her address and we could go and see her. She'd get such a surprise. Especially when she thought we were still in Dublin. Oh, there was still the missing Turner, but that would turn out to be some misunderstanding. Or something her employer had been told by Mrs Hanna. Heather had made an enemy in her, that's all.

But days passed and no word came.

My sleep began to be affected, causing a rampage in my brain. I was again getting angry at Heather. Children were meant to be running away, not parents. Why wouldn't she write? What was so hard about picking up a pen? This anger turned to depression and depression caused apathy. I had no energy for anything. Soon it'd be August, and we'd have to go back to school in September. Where was she? Our summer was ruined. We hadn't even gone on one of those bus trips round London. We had done nothing except worry about her. And what about our plans for the flat? I'd imagined it so often. The furniture. The cups and saucers. The family Christmases we'd have. Oh, we'd ask Grandfather and Brigid over. But we'd be a normal family. Maybe Dad would even come back.

But I couldn't really imagine that. Katie'd never agree to it. I could remember better times, times when he took me to the Gate Theatre. I always felt so special and idiotically boasted to everyone, "My Daddy's acting in the play." And the attendants fussed around me and let me have free coffee at the interval. I've always loved coffee since. Katie didn't have those memories, because when he was in the Gate, she was just a little young - two years is a big difference at a certain age. So she didn't have so many happy memories to balance the bad ones. So she was still violently anti-him. She was a black and white person, after all.

During this time Katie and Wally got very friendly. It wasn't anything emotional. They just liked each other. Once they went out for a pizza without me. I was too tired and didn't feel like eating, so stayed home to read. I knew they wanted to talk. I didn't care so long as he didn't let her drink. She'd gone to pot lately, smoking cigarettes all the time. And she'd had her hair cut in a skin-head style to match that leopard dress. Which she wore absolutely everywhere.

One night she didn't come home till two. I lay there, like an irate parent, imagining the worst. Now I understood Grandfather waiting up for me. It's true you have to walk in another's person's shoes before you understand. Wally shouldn't keep her out this late. Or maybe she was attacked on the way home.

At last she crept in.

I snapped on the light, shouting, "Where were you?"

She blinked nervously. "Liz took me to Jerry's flat."

"Was Wally with you?"

"No. He went home."

"You mean he left you?"

"Mind your own business!"

I jumped out of bed.

To my amazement I hit her. "You're going straight home!"

At first she was too shocked to react. Then she came for me, landing a hard slap.

I pushed her away, red with shame and pain. How could I have done that? I was just as bad as Dad. "Look, stop. I'm sorry!"

She was crying pathetically.

"I'm sorry. Now stop. Jerry's a bad man." I was out of my mind with worry.

At first she didn't answer, but at last she looked up, her eyes red. "But he gave me a hundred pounds."

"Who?"

"Jerry - LOOK!" She threw a wad of money on the bed. It was wrapped in an elastic band.

My heart stopped. Had Jerry done anything to my sister? "How'd you get home?"

"Jerry drove me."

"Did he do anything?"

"No!" She took off her dress and got into bed, sighing like a tired-out child.

I was getting angry again, but stopped myself. "Well, you're giving this back. He'll want his pound of flesh."

"He said it's to help find Heather!"

I pulled on my dressing gown. "Where is he now?"

She said he was upstairs in Liz's room.

So I ran up and knocked on the door.

"Come in!" Liz shouted.

As usual, the room reeked of perfume and stale cigarette smoke. Liz was dressed to kill and doing her eyes up at the mirror while Jerry waited. He sat on the bed, smoking. It smelled funny and I guessed it was something illegal - maybe hash. As usual his spivvy suit was completely out of character with his rough face and hands. "What is it, love?"

I put the envelope down on the bed. "We can't take this."

He handed it back to me, blowing smoke from the side of his mouth. "Look on it as a loan."

I shook my head. "We'd never be able to pay it back."

He smirked. "Well you can work it off."

I stood my ground. "No, thanks!"

He smirked again, lowering his voice. "Listen love, there's money to be made in London. You needn't slave here for pennies. I can set the two of you up."

"Sorry, we're not leaving William Shakespeare's." I made for the door.

"Wait love!" he came after me. "Liz told me your old lady's missing."

"Yes," I said quickly. "I'm going to the police!"

"I wouldn't do that, love."

I searched his face. "But why?"

"Cos, it'll do her no good. Take the word of an old pro. She'll go down for stealing a painting."

Maybe Jerry was right? Maybe I'd done the right thing all along? Maybe I wasn't so thick? But I wasn't taking his money. It wasn't difficult to imagine what he had in mind. I was green, but not that green. I'd seen Liz's bruises. I knew he was some sort of pimp.

Sixteen

But we couldn't go on in Limbo. We couldn't do nothing forever. Perhaps Katie was right and Heather was being persecuted. How else could you explain the phone call, and the letter and funny chocolates? Why else would she treat us like this? Or else she had amnesia or something. Or was in some hospital from not eating. Or maybe her ulcer was back. She might need us. I knew the kind of food to make her better, mashed potatoes and stewed chicken. July was almost over and we'd done nothing.

But we did have some definite clues: the chocolates. We'd kept them for evidence. So the next payday, I put both our wages in an envelope. Then I went back to A Beresford Clarke, the detective, with the chocolates. Surely he'd see they were tampered with and help?

There was the same ritual about getting in.

He looked a bit surprised to see me as I came into the untidy office. "Hello, you again?"

I smiled agreeably. I'd washed my hair and worn my best clothes - a denim midi and white blouse. Maybe I could get him to like me ... Maybe charm would work. It's amazing how you compromise your principles.

He looked even more dissipated, his pink face a contrast to the brown wings of hair. He scratched the back of his neck and his tummy bulged behind a yellow waistcoat. "I wondered what happened to you two. Paddies at large and that."

If anything we were Patricias. The English were really dense.

"We've changed jobs. To a pub."

"I thought you might have gone back to Granny."

"Grandfather." I put our money on the table. "There's a hundred pounds there. It's enough for five hours. Will you please help us?"

He blew out his pudgy cheeks and made a tent with his stubby fingers. "Do you take me for a sap?"

I pushed the envelope across the table.

He didn't pick it up, just kept looking at me. "Did

you steal that?"

"No! It's our wages." Keeping my patience, I took out the chocolates. "We got these sweets in the post. They look funny."

He glanced at them. "Hmm ... what's this? The Case of the Poison Chocolates? You're not very original, are you?"

"What do you mean?"

"I mean there's a thriller called *The Case of the Poison Chocolates*."

"Someone sent them to us," I said.

"People send girls sweets. Normal girls! Look, you and your sister are crazy. I wish you'd go away." He swivelled around in his chair, and got up.

I started crying. Anything made me cry now. I was going to bits.

"Women!" he shouted, sitting down again.

I wiped my eyes. "Sorry!"

"Of all the gin joints in all the towns in all the world she has to walk into mine!" he muttered in his gravelly mock-American. He sat looking at me then spoke in his own voice. "Listen, your Ma's mislaid, she'll turn up."

I liked him when he spoke like that. It was crazy, but I was getting a sort of crush. I don't know why, but I fell for all sorts of weird people. Always older. Like the priest who taught us RE And Grandfather's doctor. And our dentist. It worried me that I had a streak of Brigid in me.

I passed him our letter. "We got this from her."

He looked at it. "See! She went somewhere in a hurry. That's no reason to think she's missing."

"I know, but she hasn't written. What if she's in danger?"

He just smiled.

"But what about the hate note?"

He kept smiling.

"And the phone call and these chocolates?"

"Miss Marple sent them," he said. "I'm surprised she hasn't bought a trench coat."

"If you mean Katie, she didn't!"

He leaned back in his chair, cupping his hands behind his bald head. "Listen, you should forget all this. Enjoy London. Have you done any sightseeing?"

I told him we'd seen the Tower from outside.

"Well, you should go in. Live your own life! Forget about your Ma. What's the name of your gin joint?"

I told him.

He wrote it down. "I know it. It's down on the river. I'll drop down for a drink."

No matter what, he wouldn't take the money. Maybe he was right and the sweets had been sent by some admirer. But who? Maybe things were getting to me. But why hadn't Heather written again? Anyhow we were back in Limbo. I knew now what kind of place that was. It was a dream state where, although you try to walk, you never make any progress. You're permanently stuck. Like all the poor babies who die before they're baptised. Hell would be better. It's a definite state.

Seventeen

They were so nice at William Shakespeare's, I probably shouldn't mention what happened next. They were like family, so it isn't really fair. I mean, people might be put off the place. That's if they go to London. But it has a bearing on our story, so I must. Living by the Thames was lovely, but there was one problem: rats basically. Big brown monsters wandered in from the river in search of food. From History I knew rats had carried the Black Death before the Fire of London. They were unhygienic and promulgated disease. So exterminators came regularly. And all food was locked in a fridge in a cage in a big walk-in pantry. In the case of an emergency, ie, a rat on the premises, our job was to distract the customers and call the manager who was an expert with a shovel.

There'd been a scare once, which Katie saw. Usually they came at night and never into my bar. But one evening, I was carrying drinks to two Americans in the upstairs restaurant. They were typical tourists, loud and kind and slow. The man wore wild plaid trousers and the woman had a blue rinse and a matching blue pants suit.

"Honey, ah gotta see St Paul's," she nagged, as I approached.

He groaned, putting his bald head in his hands. "St Paul's what?"

"St Paul's Cath-ee-dral."

"Christ, another goddam church!"

I smiled at the comment. I could just picture the kind of summer the poor man was having. But then my face froze as a big fat rat scuttled from under their table and headed for the far corner of the room.

I just stood there.

It was the size of a kitten.

"Are they our drinks, hon?" the woman asked.

I still couldn't move.

"Honey! We're here."

"Oh!" I put down the rattling tray. Luckily it was early, so they were the only people in the restaurant.

"I asked for Bourbon on the rocks, hon," the man said.

I looked at him vaguely. "Rocks?"

"Yeah, on the rocks. Not straight-up."

"Straight up?" I repeated, my eye on the corner.

"He means ice, honey." The woman smiled kindly at me, then turned on her husband. "Jeez, Ray! She doesn't know what rocks are!"

"Sorry, hon. Bring me a few ice cubes."

"Ice cubes, of course ... " My eyes were riveted on the rat. It was sniffing at the legs of a sideboard.

Then Mr Williams, the manager, passed, hearing the American's request. "Get the gentleman some ice, Clare."

Turning my back to them, I grimaced at Mr Williams. Somehow I had to get him to see the rat. "Will I LOOK in the corner?"

He frowned irately. "Look in the corner? No, it's in the freezer!"

The rat jumped onto the cheese board.

I made another face. "I'll LOOK on the cheeseboard, then."

He just looked puzzled. "The ice is in the kitchen freezer!"

I tried again. How could he be so stupid? "Will I need a SHOVEL?"

"Ray! See what a darn fuss you've made!" the woman drawled.

The husband looked abashed. "I only asked for ice."

"He wants ice, Clare!" Mr Williams shouted, doing a sort of irascible Basil Fawlty dance. "Ice!"

I made a frantic face. But he still didn't get it. I put on my theatrical voice. "I'll use the SHOVEL!"

"The shovel?" Mr Williams' eyes darted to the sideboard.

The thin edge of the wedge became a plank in his brain.

The rat was on its hindlegs, nibbling happily.

He sprang into action, grabbing the Bourbon from the table and handing it to me.

It dropped.

There was glass and whiskey everywhere.

"Say, that's my drink!" The American stood up furious.

"You stupid girl!" Mr Williams shouted. "Get the customer another drink, at once!" Then to the Americans, "You can't get decent staff nowadays! It's impossible. Impossible. The drinks are on the house. And I'm moving you to another table."

I looked flustered. "I'm very sorry ...!"

"It's all right, hon," the woman comforted. "See what you've done, Ray!"

But he was still annoyed. "We're OK here. Just bring me a drink!"

But Mr Williams whisked up the other drink, cutlery and tablecloth. Then ushered them out to the bar with as much noise and fuss as possible. "I must insist. No! Follow me, please! Good! That's it!"

"Now look here," the man protested.

But he was almost pushed through the door.

They were resettled at a table in one of the downstairs bars and the restaurant was closed for the evening. Inside I heard loud banging, but the rat escaped into the pantry cage. Still, the panic was over. It would be found later and executed.

Back in my bar, Mr Williams hugged me. "Brilliant girl! You saved the day!"

And the American woman felt so sorry for me she gave me a huge tip - £5.

But that's not all.

When Katie heard what happened, she just said, "Wait a moment." Then ran down the lane to our house and got the famous box of chocolates. "Now we'll see," she whispered.

Then, when no one was looking, she slid one quickly into the pantry. "Now we'll know."

We did.

When we were finishing up, Mr Williams came into my bar looking puzzled. "About that problem -."

I was drying a glass. "You got the rat?"

"No." He took the money out of my till. "But it's curious, very curious."

"What?"

"It died, Clare. But there was no poison out. I've checked with chef."

We were back at Go.

Eighteen

All that summer I swung between two poles, anger at Heather and fear she was in danger. Now I was afraid again. Had our chocolates poisoned the rat? Or had something else? They certainly weren't normal sweets. Also I had a feeling of *déjà-vu*. All my nightmares were coming true. We were surrounded by rats, literally and metaphorically. If the sweets were poisoned, the letter had been real and so had the phone call. Heather must be in some sort of trouble. What had happened? And who on earth was trying to harm us? Who?

Katie still swore it was Mrs Hanna. She had sent the letter, phoned us and then posted us chocolates. Every night in bed she went through litanies of possibilities.

"She thinks we'll find out she's the thief."

I concentrated on my book. All summer I'd been trying to finish the Sartre book, but was getting nowhere. With all that had been happening, my concentration had gone to hell.

"Don't you think she looks evil?"

I kept on reading.

"Well ... she didn't seem to like us."

"She's a witch."

True, she'd seen us walking down the street that day. And for no reason, she'd chased us madly with an umbrella. So she could've sent the note and the chocolates. Anything was possible. Anything. I know that now.

My sister was still typically all for action. Now she talked wildly of disguising herself as a cleaner, or some official like a gasmeter reader and gaining entry to the Walton Street house. She was sure she'd find clues to our mother's whereabouts. Or to the picture's.

"Shut up," I always said.

Katie was really a handful. As the 'sensible' one, I had to keep my head. But I had to do something. I couldn't go on dithering - that was OK for Hamlet. He was only a character in a play, whereas we were in real life. I couldn't think of anything else, so I tried the detective again.

He listened to my account of the rat poisoning with his tongue literally in his cheek. Then he rolled his eyes. "When are you going to stop telling stories?"

I felt myself reddening - it was always the same response. Who would ever believe us? I groped in my bag, taking out the box. "Would you please have these chocolates examined?"

"Do you take me for a sap?"

"But you're meant to help people!"

"That's usually my business."

"What's so unusual about us?"

He guffawed. "A crank phone call would be bad enough. But poison chocolates and a hate note as well! Really."

I looked at the ground. Was it our fault?

"Next you'll be telling me that someone's following you. Has your sister suggested that?"

Suddenly tears came into my eyes. I was sick of people not believing us. I didn't even care if he saw me crying now.

He put his head in his hands. "Oh, Mother of God, is this the end of Rico?"

But he didn't say one thing to console me. He just sat there staring at me with hard blue eyes. Finally I got up to go.

He barred my way. "Oh, wait a minute."

"No!"

"You're an OK kid. Ever had an Indian meal?"

So we ended up in an Indian restaurant. I knew he liked me, really. I felt sort of more grown up. He told me his initial A stood for Alan and I was to call him that. I agreed to, although I never have. But I'll always remember being brought out by him. It was my first Indian meal and my first time in a restaurant with someone old. He must be years older than Wally.

He offered me a glass of beer, but I wouldn't break my pledge not to drink. So he ordered all sorts of exotic things from the big menu. Papadoms, a yogurt mix, chicken curry, yellow rice and chutneys. It was delicious. I was sorry Katie was missing it.

I kept bringing up our problems. But he always cut me off with a comment about the food. Once he said, "Tell me about yourself."

I told him I liked astronomy.

"Well, astronomy is looking up."

I smiled at his joke. "And I want to be an actor."

He held up his beer glass. "Here's looking at you, kid."

"You've seen too many films," I said.

"And you've read too many detective stories."

"I've only read one in my life!"

"What was that?"

"*Brat Farrar* by Josephine Tey. Grandfather gave it to me when I had the flu."

He lit a cigarette. "Don't worry, your Ma will turn up. You'll get another letter one of these days. In the meantime, you should go home to Granny - eh, Grandad. You'll feel safer there."

I said nothing. He really believed we'd invented the whole thing.

While we waited for the coffee, he said, "I suppose you have a boyfriend?"

I nodded, telling him all about Wally's brains.

He snorted. "More important, is he wise?"

I shrugged. "Oh, I think so."

He blew out curls of smoke. "I suppose you're RC?"

I thought for a minute. "No, I'm DA."

"What's that?"

"Definite Agnostic."

"That's a contradiction in terms."

I made sandcastles with the sugar.

"I suppose you've slept with him?" he asked.

I reddened, he was weird. "Well - I'm still in school. It's not really like that."

"You're afraid of letting your family down?"

I laughed. It was the silliest thing I'd ever heard. Wally and I had tried it once, but stopped half way. According to a book he gave me, you were meant to reach a plateau state. But I didn't. What did everybody see in it? He'd got guilty about it, because of my age, so we decided not to try again till I was eighteen. Which was OK with me. I didn't want to be lumbered with a baby, especially one that might look like Wally. I already had Katie and Heather to take care of. "I don't have a family, except my sister," I said with some sarcasm. "And, if you remember, we've lost a vital member." I hesitated. "Are you married?"

"I was."

"Oh!" I looked away. A plot was hatching in my brain. I'd have done anything for his help. He liked me, I knew, but wouldn't try anything because of my age. I felt sure of that. But I could make him jealous. So I told him about Jerry's offer of a hundred pounds, saying, "He gave it to Katie in an envelope."

He threw down his napkin. "For what?"

"To help us pay you. He said I could work it off."

"On your back! Who is this man?"

I told him about Liz. And about Katie going to that party and coming in so late.

"That's no way to behave! I hope you told your awful little sister off!"

"Oh, I did."

"Don't associate with people like that!"

"I wasn't!"

He rubbed the back of his neck worriedly. "You've heard of AIDS?"

I nodded, looking away. We'd had a talk on it in

school.

He went on and on about the disease. How you die and that. I was glad no one else was in the restaurant. Afterwards he cooled down and walked me back to the Underground. "Why don't you forget all this and enjoy the summer?"

I didn't answer. Forget? It was idiotic. How could you possibly forget your own mother? Anymore than you could forget your name or your self. At the station he said, "You know your way home from here?"

"Yes, I can read the map." I was too ashamed to make eye contact. My attempt to get his help had been an utter failure.

But he kissed me on the forehead. "You're an OK kid. You know what?"

"What?"

"We'll always have Paris!"

He laughed, but I didn't know what he was talking about. It was probably another boring film.

He stood there giggling stupidly to himself.

"It's not exactly funny," I said.

He grimaced, scratching his wing of hair. "Oh! ... Give me your poisoned sweeties! I'll prove you're both bananas!"

He took them from me and walked away waving his fingers like Charlie Chaplin.

If we were bananas, he was nuts.

Nineteen

We called the detective ABC, or A for short. He was right. We soon got another letter from Heather.

My dear Girls,
Please forgive my delay in writing. I know you are wondering about my long silence and were probably very disappointed about the last minute change in plans. Believe me it was unavoidable.
For the last six months, I've been plagued by a certain person who shall for the moment be nameless. This person has made life complicated for me. So your summer had to be postponed. We will definitely get together next year. I got myself into a mess, my darlings. Time alone will mend it. In the meantime, be patient with your poor old mother. I love you both very much,
Heather.

Grandfather had sent it on.
Katie grabbed the envelope.
I read it again. What was the "mess"? It had to be the stolen picture. So it was true. And who had made life "complicated"? Mrs Hanna? Heather was definitely in some sort of trouble. But at least she wasn't avoiding us. She just didn't know we were in London. And thought we were safely with Grandfather. She was probably planning to see us at Christmas or next summer. Maybe we could get the flat then. But we couldn't wait that long. It seemed like an eternity away.
"There's no address," I said.
Katie was studying the envelope. "It was posted in

Maidenhead. Ten days ago."

Liz told us Maidenhead was a posh town in the Thames stockbroker belt. We still didn't know her address, but at least we'd narrowed the field of search. Heather was probably working somewhere as a nurse or companion. But was she in a private house, or a nursing home? We were off work the next day, so headed for Paddington Station where we got a train west. I don't know what we expected. Going on spec was a symptom of our desperation. We had a sort of cracked fantasy that if we walked around we'd bump into her. Out shopping or something. Anyhow it was comforting to be near her. To be breathing the same air. And we were doing something at last.

It was a fairly nice place. Tidy like everything English, but cold, cold, cold. As we walked round the town, a line from a poem kept echoing in my head,

> *I would that my heart could utter*
> *the thoughts that arise in me.*

There was no one to ask anything. In an Irish town you'd be able to enquire in a shop if there were hospitals or nursing homes in the area. But here people just looked at you funnily. So we wandered aimlessly up and down the High Street and into leafy Victorian suburbs. Then we found poorer streets and a redbricked Victorian school. But we didn't even know what kind of a house we were looking for. It was stupid to walk around like some sort of zombies from outer space. Finally we went and bought fish and chips and went down to the river to eat them.

We sat on a bench watching houseboats tug at their moorings. Beneath them the Thames flowed inexorably, ignoring this world's troubles. And the trees reflected greenly in the deep peaceful water.

"We're getting warm," Katie said. "She must be here somewhere."

I watched a branch floating in the river. "We're like that branch."

"I don't see any branch."

I pointed to it. "It's a symbol of us."

She frowned. "You mean a simile."

"It's a symbol."

"You said 'like.' That's a simile."

"A symbol's a type of simile."

She walked huffily to the water's edge. "You think you know so much! A branch is a branch!"

I kept on arguing. I was trying to annoy her, because I was so upset myself. "No, it's not!"

"What is it then?" She almost spat the words at me.

"You just perceive it as a branch. It's atoms really."

"Oh, shut up!"

"Oh, shut up! That's really brilliant, you know!" I was being horrible. Why couldn't she argue intelligently? But maybe we were perceiving things wrongly now. Maybe there was nothing wrong with Heather being missing. Maybe it was OK for things to be so upside down. Why was it so abnormal for parents and not children to run away? Maybe they were running away from us. Maybe they didn't want us. This idea made me feel bad about fighting with Katie - I was still ashamed of myself for hitting her. We always fought when we got fed up. And we were very fed up now.

There was an angry silence between us. I followed her to the water's edge. "Maybe we should go back to London."

She wouldn't look at me.

"Come on," I said. "Let's go back to the station."

"No! I'm going to enquire."

"Where?" I knew the look in her eye. She got defiant

Has Anyone Seen Heather?

when I was mean to her. I wanted to walk away, but couldn't. If I left her alone, she'd get into trouble. She'd definitely get arrested in her leopard mini and skinhead hairstyle. So I said gently. "What'll you say? Has anyone seen Heather?"

"We could show them her photo," she persisted. "Or ask if there's a hospital in the area."

"But her hair might be different now. She could be thinner."

I was nervous about talking to strangers. Especially, after Piccadilly. But there was no stopping Katie. Sometimes I think there's something wrong with her brain. I really do.

We went into a supermarket on the High Street and showed our photo to a girl cashier, asking if she'd seen anyone like Heather coming into the shop. She had pink hair and blinked long lashes at us. "Can't say I've seen her, love. Who is she?"

"Our mother," Katie said. "She's living somewhere here. She might be in a hospital."

"What kind of a hospital?"

"We don't know. She's missing."

My sister was really brilliant.

"Hmm ..." The girl looked us up and down suspiciously. "Why not go to the police?"

I made for the door. It was always the same answer: the police, the police, the police.

"The station's down the street, love," the girl called kindly.

Just then the manager came over, staring at us coldly. "What's going on here?"

I pulled Katie on, starting to run.

"Hey!" he called, looking at the girl. "Hey, come back!"

But we fled. God, why was he angry? Did he think

we were shoplifters or something?

On the way to the station, we went into a chemist shop. Katie reasoned that Heather might go in there to get a prescription filled. After all, this would be part of her job. I argued against it, but it was no use. So I bought some toothpaste. Then Katie casually showed the attendant our photo. He was pale and spotty and for some reason looked terrified. He held the photo tremblingly, "No, I don't remember anyone like this."

As he gave it back I asked, "Are there any mental hospitals in the area?"

"No ... " He took a quick breath and pressed a bell.

As we left, an older woman appeared.

"I'll call the police," she hissed in our wake.

I suppose our question was suspicious. But did we really look that dangerous?

Near the station we passed a second-hand shop with notices in the window. They were ads for flats and baby-sitters. The man in the shop was nice for a change and allowed us to place one for Heather.

Twenty

When we heard nothing from that, we advertised in *The Maidenhead Advertiser*.

DESPERATELY SEEKING HEATHER KELLY.
Ring Clare and Katie at O71-402-7777

Has Anyone Seen Heather?

It wasn't very original, but it was all we could think of. And the wording from the Madonna movie might catch someone's eye. As it was cheaper than the London papers, we had it put in big print. Maybe she'd see it. Or someone would tell her about it. Heather made friends easily. She must know people in Maidenhead by now. Two days later Mr Williams popped his head into my bar. "Phone, Clare! Take it in the office!"

I nearly died. "Eh - who is it?"

"Dunno, some woman."

My heart seemed to stop beating. It had to be Heather. Oh, God ... I tried to keep calm and walked upstairs slowly, rehearsing what I'd say. How could she behave like this? What kind of a mother was she? We were six weeks looking for her. Six damn weeks.

"Hello!" I snapped into the receiver.

"Clare! Darling, where are you?"

I lost my voice.

"Clare? Are you there?"

I tried to breathe. "Yes -."

"It's Heather."

"I know."

"Darling, you're not very talkative. I rang -."

"Sorry!" I tried to keep from crying. "You saw our ad?"

"What ad?"

"We advertised in *The Maidenhead Advertiser* ..."

"You what? I didn't see it. No, I was trying to tell you I rang your Grandfather."

We were up creeksville now.

"And he told me you'd come to London!"

I couldn't speak.

"Where are you, Clare? I thought you were with Grandfather."

I got my breath.

"Clare?"

"Yes."

"Why didn't you stay with Grandad?"

"We thought you wanted us. We came over in June."

"Oh dear ..."

There was a pause.

I broke it. "Does Grandfather know we didn't meet you? If so, he'll be upset."

"No," Heather said quickly, "I covered up. When he said, in his usual accusing way, `I thought they were with you!' I immediately said, `Oh, they are! I've just temporarily mislaid their number. And they were talking about going back to Dublin. I thought they might've already left."

"Did he believe it?"

"I think so. He gave me a lecture about carelessness. And not looking after you properly. He never changes does he? Where are you now?"

"We're working in a Southwark Inn - William Shakespeare's. We came over in June."

"But didn't you get my letter?"

"No. It went astray."

"Oh, God!"

"It's OK. We've been worried about you."

"How did you know I was in Berkshire?"

"The postmark on your letter. Can we come and see you?"

She hesitated. "It's awkward, darling."

What did she mean, awkward? "But we want to come."

"Darling, it's not -. I'd prefer to meet you in London."

I couldn't believe it. "But we're meant to be a family!"

She sighed. "Of course, we're a family. How's Katie?"

I couldn't speak. I was choking with anger.

"Clare, please answer me. How's Katie?"

"She wants to see you," I kept my voice level. "Can't we come down?"

She hesitated again. "I'm sort of lying low, darling."

"Please!"

"Well ... if you must. I'm at the Maidenhead Nursing Home. It's on Raymond Road."

So she wasn't really missing. It had been a mix-up, after all. Just like A Beresford Clarke predicted. All the advertising had been in vain. She'd turned up in the most normal way. But why didn't she want to see us? She sounded so odd, I thought it must be true about the picture. There was nothing for it but to make her give it back. Then sneak her back to Ireland as soon as we got paid again. Maybe Grandfather would take her in. But had she really fooled him? Was it possible? The next thing, Grandfather could be over, dragging us back.

Twenty-one

We found Heather the next day. By a bit of juggling and thanks to the kindness of Liz, we got time off. As the Maidenhead train pulled out of Paddington, I stared glumly at the endless high rise flats. London was sometimes so sordid and depressing. Finding Heather was our greatest wish. Yet I had a terrible feeling of anti-climax. What would we find out? So many questions came into my head. Was she working at the Maidenhead Home, or was she a patient? Was it a mental hospital? Would she be desperately thin? Why wasn't she keen to see us?

Katie sat opposite me. She'd washed what was left of her hair and wore her leopard mini. She was about a stone heavier and her tummy stuck out. I didn't tell her to hold it in. She already looked too nervous, as if she were meeting Heather for the first time. As if Heather were a stranger.

She caught my stare. "Do you think she'll be glad to see us?"

"Of course, she will."

"But she left us."

"She had to."

"She could've come back."

I said nothing. It was true.

"Maybe she never wanted to," Katie persisted.

I sighed boredly. "Of course she did."

Of course, of course, of course. But I wasn't so sure. Our parents were peculiar. Obviously they'd regretted us. Why else would they leave us? After all, Dad had never even written. How could he do that?

The address we were given was on the outskirts of the town. We found it easily by asking directions. The house looked typical of those redbrick Victorian mansions you saw all over the outskirts of London. A sign outside said: MAIDENHEAD NURSING HOME.

Walking up the leafy avenue, Katie whispered, "I'm going to be sick."

"Take a deep breath."

She did.

"Is that better?"

"I think so."

I was just as nervous, but wouldn't admit it. I

wanted to be "the sensible one" to my sister. But I pitied her at that moment. God, she'd known so little of her parents. Only rows and screaming. In a way she'd been robbed of childhood. And now she was nervous about meeting her own mother. It wasn't fair.

The entrance door was open. The antiseptic hospital smell made me queasier. We walked into a big flagged hall where a porter sat reading at a desk.

I went over. "We've come to see Mrs Heather Kelly."

He checked a list. "Take the lift to the third floor."

We did. As we stepped out a grim-looking nurse was standing by a window, studying charts. "Can I help you?" she enquired.

"We're looking for Heather Kelly," I said.

She perused us. "It's not visiting hours."

I shifted nervously. So Heather was a patient. "We won't stay long."

"She's in number 15." She led the way up the corridor, carrying a chart. "Please be quick."

"We will," I said.

"We're her children," Katie grumbled.

"I don't want her worried." The nurse walked on grimly, stopping at a closed door. She showed us into a room with two beds.

As we went in, Heather came out of a bathroom. She wore a blue wool dressing-gown. Her skin was wrinkly and her hair roots were now completely white where the blonde had grown out. Also she was thin. So she had her anorexia again. "Clare! Katie!"

We went to her awkwardly.

She hugged us, then stood back. "Let me look at you! Katie, you're so grown up! "

My sister blushed like a big shy child.

"Oh, Clare, give me a proper hug!"

They say time stands still. It does. That was the

happiest moment, no, the happiest second of my life. And it seemed the longest. Heather's smile was the same. Her eyes as blue.

"Do I look a sight?"

"No!" we said together.

She led us to chairs. "Sister, these are my girls."

"It's not visiting hours," she grumped.

"They've come a long way!" my mother said.

We sure had.

The nurse went to the door. "I suppose we can bend the rules. Don't go getting worked up now."

She sat on the bed opposite us. "I just want to look at you. Katie, I can't believe the size of you! You're as big as a house now. And Clare, still as thin."

All my anger vanished. I wanted to take her away from that place and home to Ireland. Grandfather would relent and look after her. "You should've told us you were ill," I said.

She frowned, wearily raking her blonde shoulder-length hair - it was a gesture of hers. "I couldn't worry you -."

"You haven't been eating," I accused.

"Now that's not true. I'm nearly eight stone."

"But why didn't you tell us you were ill?"

"Clare, I told you - I couldn't worry you. I've done nothing else all my life."

She was daft. It was much more worrying to be in the dark. I told her how we came in early June. How we expected her to be at Euston. Then we'd gone to her job when she didn't turn up.

She pulled a face. "I suppose you met Mrs Hanna."

Then Katie let it out about the missing picture.

Our mother was aghast. Again she ran her fingers through her hair. "My God! She didn't say I stole it?"

Relief ran through me like a drug. "They both did.

Mr Livingstone too."

"But how ridiculous! I was bringing it back."

I panicked again. "But where is it now?"

She hesitated, before going on. "I suppose I should tell you everything."

"Yes!" we said together.

She looked from one of us to the other. "I was desperate for money, so I pawned it for a hundred pounds. I needed money for you two. I wanted to see you so much."

We looked at each other in alarm.

"Oh, don't look like that!" She raked her hair again. "I was bringing it back!"

So it was true. But at least she wanted us to come. She wanted us. That made up for everything. All the weeks of waiting. Everything.

"Before I could retrieve it, I left Mr Livingstone's. The ticket was with my things. I rang, but they refused to send them on."

"Did you ask Mr Livingstone?"

"No! I rang that horrible old cow - Mrs Hanna. But she hung up on me."

There was something rotten in the state of Denmark.

"I'll collect it," I said. Dammit, they'd no right to keep her stuff. How could she bring back the picture?

Heather was saying over and over, "How could Mr Livingstone believe that I wouldn't bring it back?" She bit her lip worriedly. "I'll tell you what happened. The painting hung in a dark corner of the library. It had been in Mr Livingstone's family for donkey's years. I kept telling him it looked like a Turner. It was sort of murky - you know the way an old painting looks. Finally he said I could have it valued. Which I did. They told me it was genuine. Although deteriorated. Due to the pigment Turner used. And damp in his studio during the last years of his life."

"They have some in the National Gallery," Katie said.

We'd gone there on a school outing.

"How much was it worth?" I asked.

She raised her eyebrows. "About twenty-five thousand pounds. I pawned it on the way home."

I said nothing. Why had she complicated her life?

"Where was the pawn shop?" Katie asked.

Heather sighed. "It was near Victoria Station. I only intended to leave it a little while. Clare, don't look like that!"

"I'm not. It's OK."

"I needed the money for you two."

My love for her was like the ocean. "I know."

"You see, Mr Livingstone was away," she went on. "He regularly goes to the country. I was going to retrieve it before he came home. Dad was going to give me the money."

"You're not back together?" I asked quickly.

She shifted awkwardly. "Only occasionally. For dinner. I lent him some money. He had a bed-sit down here. I was transferred because of it. He'll be dying to see you girls."

I said nothing. Why didn't I guess that he'd let her down. It was the old story.

Heather sighed. "As far as Mr Livingstone knew, it was only being valued."

"He said that was OK?" I quizzed.

"Yes, but then I was carted off to hospital."

We both stared in alarm.

She held up her hand. "Now, don't look like that. I'm all right now. It was just my ulcer. It started bleeding and I collapsed - on the way back from posting my letter to you. I was brought to St George's Hospital. I was there for a month and then transferred down here."

"You got sick because you gave up eating!" I said crossly.

"Clare, I'm as fat as a fool now." She puffed out her cheeks.

"You're still underweight," I said sternly.

"You should've told us you were sick!" Katie said.

"I know. I thought you'd be with Grandad. I was afraid to ring him. He's such a misery."

Katie reddened. "But I love Grandad."

Heather gave me a quick look. "I know, darling. But he just never lays off me. Now be fair, does he?"

It was true. He was awful about Heather, saying, even behind her back, that her troubles were all her own fault.

"He didn't want us to come to London either," I said.

Heather laughed, saying in a mock posh accent. "It's not a place for nice young ladies. He'd have a fit if he knew you were working in a pub! Katie's surely too young?"

"She's in the restaurant."

My mother went on in a low voice. "Don't judge me, children. Please! The irony is, I was tempted to steal it - he has so much money! But I didn't!"

"Mrs Hanna must want you in his bad books. Otherwise, she'd give you your stuff." I said slowly.

"She's always been a queer fish," Heather went on. "Mr Livingstone created the problem by liking me a bit better."

So Katie had been right - *cherchez la femme*. I rooted in my bag. "She's been bothering us too. We got this in the post."

Heather put on her battered horn-rimmed glasses and read it aloud slowly. "As you value your life and reason, stay away from London." She pulled a face then peered at us over the lens. "Well ... she must've gone completely bonkers."

The we told her about the phone call and the chocolates.

She looked at us oddly. "Are you sure it's not some practical joke?"

I shook my head. "Katie gave one to a rat. It died."

Heather shrieked with laughter. She has a wonderful hooting laugh. "Where did she get the rat?"

Katie laughed too. It was funny really. "They come into the pub all the time. Usually they have professional rat poisoners."

Heather looked at us aghast. Then studied the note again. "But why didn't you bring this to the police?"

She certainly didn't sound guilty.

I smiled at Katie. "Because we thought they were after you."

Heather raised her eyebrows. "After me? Oh dear, I suppose they are now."

Then the nurse came back with some white medicine in a glass. "Time for this, Heather."

Heather took it, grimacing. "My cocktail!"

"Drink it all, now!"

She sipped a little. "Ugh!"

When the door was shut again, Heather put her medicine down on the table. "It might be tricky if they nail me. Perhaps I should get a solicitor."

I touched her hand. "We'll retrieve the picture. We have the money. Then bring it back to Mr Livingstone. We'll tell him you did it for us. That you're down here now."

Heather rinsed the remainder of her medicine down the sink.

"Shouldn't you take it all?" I said worriedly. She never took care of herself.

"No. It's revolting!" Heather looked at us both sadly. "I've missed my girls so much." Again she raked her hair worriedly. "I'm a rotten mother."

I hugged her again. "No, you're not. Everything was too hard." Then I remembered something. "By the way, who was the person in your letter?"

She frowned. "What person?"

"You mentioned someone `complicating' your life. In your letter."

She looked slowly from one to the other. "That was your father."

"Dad?" we both said.

There was an awkward silence, during which we looked at each other.

I broke it. "But you said you're not getting back together."

Heather sighed. "He's in Scotland for a few weeks. Then he'll be in London. He's been getting work lately. You might as well know - he wants to come back. Permanently. He's on the dry now, Clare. He's joined AA." She looked from one of us to the other. "Well, what do you think?"

Katie's upper lip trembled. "No way!"

Then I mentioned our plans. "We were thinking the same thing. Maybe a flat in Dun Laoghaire. But just the three of us."

"You have to forgive people, Clare." Heather said gently.

I looked at the floor. I couldn't let Katie down. "But he locked you out with nothing on."

"I had my night-gown on," my mother said firmly. "That's your grandfather's tragedy, he'll never forgive. I'll give Dad your number. He'll be in touch. Give him a chance, please! For me."

Before I could say anything, the tea trolley was rolled

in. And the nurse said it was time to go. We had only just come. Still, I kissed Heather goodbye, whispering that I'd get the picture out and bring it back somehow. The nurse watched me suspiciously. Then she watched Katie say goodbye. What was she looking at?

Back out in the corridor, she repeated her warning. "Your mother's been very ill. I don't want her worried."

What were we to do? Disappear from the earth? Anyhow it was the other way around. Heather had really worried us by not writing. Because of her, it had been a horrible summer. But then we weren't a normal family. We were like Halley's Comet, the opposite to the universe.

Twenty-two

All the way back in the train, I pondered on the ordinary solution to our problem. Ordinary compared to what'd been happening. Everything was normal really. Heather had pawned the painting for us. She loved us after all. Otherwise she wouldn't have done it. And she didn't know she was missing or that we were in England. If she hadn't written, it was for a good reason: illness. Brought on by nerves and fear of Grandfather finding out about Dad. Grandfather had never approved of the marriage and since it got violent had the satisfaction of being right. There'd be ructions if he knew they'd patched it up. He was an absolute prophet of doom. "If a man beats a woman once, he'll do it again," he always said. But maybe they'd have a chance if Dad wasn't drinking? I was torn. I wanted us to be a family again, yet I didn't trust him. But Heather said you have to forgive.

You have to forgive, I told myself in time with the train's motion homeward. You have to forgive. After all I had hit Katie too. Humpty dumpty. You have to forgive. Humpty dumpty had a great fall. They hadn't been able to put him together again. Would they be able to fix our Dad?

Now that we'd found Heather, we more or less shelved the other weird things that had happened. Mrs Hanna was a nut but did it really matter if she'd phoned us or wanted us out of London? Now we'd something tangible to do: get the picture back from the pawnshop. I had the money from our savings. But the ticket was with Heather's stuff. How were we to confront Mrs Hanna? Or get back her stuff? The woman was obviously dangerous. And mental. It was best to try and forget about what she'd done to us. If, indeed, it was her.

Katie was staring glumly out the train window, sucking her thumb.

"Cheer up!" I knew she was nervous about the future.

She kept her thumb in her mouth. "They won't want us. We'll have to go back to Grandad."

I sighed. "Maybe they'll live in Ireland."

"But will they want us?"

"Of course."

"Do you ever think about Daddy?"

"Yeah." I looked out the window too. I sure did.

"Remember when he made the snowman in the garden?" Katie's voice was dreamy. "How old was I then?"

"I don't remember that. Remember his pancakes?"

But Katie didn't. So much for being in the same family.

I thought we should try the pawnshop first. But we had no ticket which made me nervous. Maybe they'd give us back the picture without the ticket. And maybe Wally'd come with us. We phoned him, arranging to meet at St Paul's on our next halfday. We usually met him on the steps of that church, since getting jobs at the pub. We walked past interesting streets with odd names like Fish Street and Bread Street until we came to the grey dome. It remains a striking image from that Summer. An image of beauty and peace from another age. We could almost see it from across the river, set in a crown of horrible skyscrapers and reigning over London's vast indifference.

That day Wally was just a speck on the wide steps.

As we came closer, he waved a *New Statesman*.

We ran up and plonked down beside him. It took a few minutes to tell the whole story. How Heather hadn't really stolen anything, just borrowed it. How Dad had let her down about the money to get it out. Then Mrs Hanna had refused to give back her stuff. I didn't tell him about Dad coming back to her. Maybe he wouldn't, and then I'd have to explain that. He couldn't love us anyhow, or he'd never have disappeared for nearly four years.

Wally took off his glasses and cleaned them fussily. "I still think it's a case for the police. Someone was out to get you girls."

I shook my head. "We've no proof."

He laughed shortly. "Proof? You get an anonymous phone call, telling you to leave London. Then a letter and box of poisoned chocolates. That's attempted murder. At least, intention to cause bodily harm."

I stood my ground. "But what about the painting?"

"What about it?" Katie asked sharply.

"Heather pawned it. She was in the wrong."

"She's still not a thief!" Katie snapped. "They kept her stuff."

Wally's chin jutted bossily. "That's right!"

It was true: things didn't quite add up. But we'd promised Heather to collect her things. Then use the ticket to retrieve the painting. That was all we could really do. But I was crippled with nerves. I mean I'm not good at phoning people like Mrs Hanna. My mouth goes dry. We sat on the steps for a while, silently taking the afternoon sun. Every few minutes we'd discuss strategies for how to get the suitcase. Katie was for boldly knocking on the door. Wally said we should phone first. My tummy just churned over and over and over.

Then we went into the cathedral, walking around and staring in awe at the huge domed ceiling. It was breathtaking, yet I felt dead to beauty. Although surrounded by it. I imagined what it was like in the Middle Ages, when people really prayed in a church like this. They didn't have seats like we do today. I stopped by a painting of Our Lord knocking on the door of a cabin tangled with weeds - I forget the name of the artist. But I'd seen holy pictures of it. The cabin was a symbol for the human heart. My heart felt like that, choked and overgrown with loneliness and fear. Underneath was an inscription:

Behold I stand at the door and knock. If any man hear my voice, and open the door, I will come to him, and will sup with him and he with me.

If only it was true. If only there was a God to help us,

instead of vast and empty space. Sister Martin believed in one, and she wasn't a fool. That's for sure. Maybe it was true. After all, I now knew that anything could be true.

I walked around, reading inscriptions to the dead. You were such a short time on this earth. It was too late for them now. But we could still act. All Summer we'd done nothing. We'd been sort of displaced persons. Terrified out of our wits. Why should we be walked on? Why couldn't we just phone and go over like Wally suggested, knock on the door and ask for her property. After all Mrs Hanna hadn't behaved very normally to us.

The Whispering Gallery wasn't open, so we couldn't go up. At the main altar, Katie shouted, "I'm going over to get her case."

Her voice echoed loudly.

"Now?" I whispered.

"Why not?" she yelled.

There was an irritated hush from a black-frocked attendant, but it had no effect.

"Then we can get the painting! And tell the police about her notes and phone calls."

I nudged her to shut up "Let's try the pawnshop first. Maybe they'll give it to us without a ticket."

At that Katie brightened. "OK, then."

She charged outside and down the steps. "Are you coming, Wally?"

He turned to me. "I think we should do something, Clare.

I hesitated. Would they really give us the picture without a ticket?

"Remember Sartre," he said.

"OK. " Feeling sick with nerves, I followed them. Damn Sartre and his theories. I was scared. I was always scared to stand up for myself - in the Dublin cinema, leaving the Imperial, all my life. We took the Circle Line to Victoria and found the pawn shop in Victoria Street, near the station, just as Heather had said. The place was Dickensian. It had three gold orbs hanging outside, like the pawn shops in Dublin. There was expensive jewellry and silver teapots displayed in the window. We stood nervously outside, finally getting up the courage to ring a bell. A heavy-set man in a brown overall coat let us in - he looked like a retired boxer or something. Inside there was a hushed air of secrecy and discretion. Another younger man smiled from behind a huge mahogany counter, rubbing his hands like Uriah Heep in the David Copperfield film.

"Can I be of assistance?" he asked in hushed tones.

I cleared my throat. "We've come about a picture. It was left here for the sum of a hundred pounds in June. By Mrs Heather Kelly, our mother."

"Do you have the ticket?"

I sighed. "No. Our mother lost it."

"We can describe the painting," Katie said.

"Yes, it was a Turner. And murky," I said.

"Don't you have records?" Wally asked squeakily.

The man just peered at us suspiciously. Finally he said, "You'll have to talk to my colleague."

And we were shown into a little snug with a small mahogany table. It was like a mini convent parlour.

"That's a bullet-proof window," Katie said.

I told her to shut up.

"She's right," Wally whispered, fingering it.

Just then another younger man entered through a connecting door from the shop. He carried a huge book and had blond skimpy hair and blue-tinted glasses. He coughed, opening it. "Let me see, you are enquiring about a painting?"

"Yes," I said, "our mother left it in in June."

"You haven't got the date?"

I shook my head.

He ran his finger down one side of the book. "Here it is."

I put my money on the counter. "I believe we owe you one hundred pounds plus interest. What's the interest?"

He regarded me suspiciously. "I'm afraid it's not so simple. We don't hand out merchandise without the ticket."

"But our mother's lost it. She left the painting here and asked us to redeem it."

He looked us over. "This sounds highly suspicious."

"There's nothing suspicious," Wally said. "They've just lost a ticket."

The man snapped the book shut. "But I'm not at liberty to give you the painting without a pledge.

I was beginning to panic. "But we must have the picture."

He slammed shut his tome. "Then bring me the pledge! And come back before seven days. After that time we'll be at liberty to sell it."

"What do you mean?" Wally said. "It's yours, if they can't find the ticket?"

"I'm afraid so. Unless their mother swears an oath with a solicitor. Then, of course, we'd need rigorous identification. And eh - we don't deal with minors."

What were we to do now? We had to have the ticket.

The man then showed us the door. On the way out the brown-coated attendant winked at me. Why did he do that?

"I vote we go over to Walton Street and get her stuff," Katie said outside. "It must be with that. They can't refuse to give it to us."

"No they can't. Come on, Clare," Wally said.

They headed for the Underground beside Victoria Station. What could I do but follow? Walton Street was almost deserted. There were only one or two stragglers coming out of the church across the street and one or two parked cars. Everything looked so innocent and leafy with the tree in front of Number 26A waving gently in the wind. The house itself seemed to smile in the Summer afternoon sun.

As the three of us stood on the steps, my heart was going like mad. "Wally, let's not do this!"

But he rang the bell.

It was too late to turn back.

The wait was eternal.

No one came, so Wally rang again.

Still no answer.

"They must be away." I was relieved at not having to face Mrs Hanna again. We knew from our mother's letters that Mr Livingstone often went to his Scottish house, taking the staff.

"The basement window's open," Katie said.

I knew her - she was thinking we could break in.

She leaned over the railings. "I'll get in the window and open the front door."

"You will not!" I snapped.

"There's no sign of an alarm." Wally said quietly. He scanned the front of the house.

I couldn't believe my ears. What was Wally saying? He was absolutely mad. I'd always thought he was a mousey person.

I grabbed my sister. "Please, let's go!"

Wally turned to me. "It'll be OK. You wait for us at the corner."

"No!" But there was nothing I could do. My sister

had won. Anyway I was afraid to let her out of my sight. By staying with her I had control, or the illusion of control.

Wally helped Katie over the railings and she dropped cat-like to the ground. Next thing she lifted the basement window and wriggled in. The wait was agonizing. As we stood there Wally breathed heavily and I told myself our actions were justified. After all, Mrs Hanna had maligned Heather and perhaps caused her to become ill. Why should she get away with everything, while our mother suffered? If she'd given her back her property in the first place, the picture would be returned by now. We were only claiming what was rightfully hers.

At last Katie opened the front door. She was grinning idiotically. "There's nobody home."

We went into the hall. There were little drops of sweat on Wally's forehead. I was shaking. But no alarms rang.

"Come on!" Wally whispered. "Let's be quick."

We crept through the thickly carpeted hall to the stairs. Our plan was to search the upstairs bedrooms first for Heather's stuff. The ticket would be with that. The long landing window looked out to a grey flagged patio with lovely red geraniums in terracota pots. A vine grew up a huge back wall. There was even white garden furniture. Everything looked so normal. I imagined Heather reading the paper there. Or chatting with Mr Livingstone over an outdoor lunch. How had things come to this terrible pass?

Katie opened a door on the first floor. Inside was a large high bed with dark carved posts. Beside it was a table crammed with medicine bottles on top and magazines underneath. There was a TV in the corner and another door opened into a bathroom.

Has Anyone Seen Heather?

"This must be Mr Livingstone's room," I whispered. "Heather's stuff won't be here."

Wally looked very nervous. "Come on!"

He was having second thoughts.

There was a lift on that floor. Another room turned out to be a library. It had a carved wood mantelpiece and shelves full of old leather-bound books. I tiptoed over to read the titles.

"Come on, Clare!" Wally whispered. "There's nothing here."

We went to the next floor.

The first door was another bedroom. Again the furniture was big and mahogany. Heather's case was on the bed. It must be her room. I searched the drawers for a pawn ticket, but they were all empty. The case was white leather and engraved with our father's initials: JAK - John Anthony Kelly.

This relic from our childhood jolted us. Katie stared at it. "Gosh, it's Dad's."

I opened the lid. There was no sign of a ticket. Heather's clothes were packed neatly inside. Why had they not given them to her? I had always thought her very well dressed, but these clothes looked shabby. On top was a framed snap of us in our togs at Killiney Beach last Summer. I remembered the day it was taken. Heather had taken us out on the Dart train for a picnic. It was one of those rare hot happy days. The sort of day you never forget.

I passed the photo to Katie. "Remember that day?"

She stared at it sadly. "You wouldn't lend me your sunglasses."

"You lost my last pair."

"I didn't!"

"You did!"

She put the photo back on top of the case. "You never

lend me anything!"

It was so untrue. "Whose shoes are you wearing now?"

She showed me the sole. "They're worn out!"

"They weren't when you got them!"

All this time Wally was getting more and more worked up. "Have your argument later! Please!" He looked under the bed and in the wardrobe. "Come on, there's nothing else here!"

I shut the case. But as I hauled it up, one side popped open again.

Wally made nervous movements with his hands, warding off imaginary midges. "Hurry, let's get out of here!"

I shut the case again. It was too late for second thoughts. Whether Wally liked it or not, we had crossed the Rubicon into the criminal life and there was no going back. If we were caught we might be sent to a reform school. Or worse. But curiously the sight of our mother's stuff had given me courage. And the case was a poor thing, but our father's. He had a good side, before he started drinking. I remembered happy times. I did, 'Enry 'Iggins, I did. You have to forgive.

Wally was at the door. His cold feet were now blocks of ice. "Come on, Clare!"

Katie ran out to the hall and opened another bedroom door. "No! We've got to find the ticket."

I followed with the case.

"No!" Wally said. "We're going!"

But there was no controlling my sister. "It must be here."

This bedroom had to be Mrs Hanna's. It had the same style furniture as Heather's, but was obviously occupied.

There were clothes scattered on a chair and hair

brushes and face creams, etc, on a tall chest of drawers.

Katie opened one of the drawers. "There might be something in here."

There were only neatly folded clothes inside.

Wally picked something from the bedside table. "It's a map of London. She's marked an X on it."

Katie stared at it suspiciously. "Why'd she do that?"

I didn't think anything of it.

Wally put it back, saying fussily, "It's time we were going."

Katie grabbed the map. "Let's keep this."

"Put it back, Katie!" I whispered.

She obeyed, then went over to the big wardrobe and looked inside. "There might be something in here."

Wally paced to the door. "It's time we were going. Clare, I'm sorry I got involved in this!"

Katie rooted in the bottom of the wardrobe, pulling out a large square frame wrapped in brown paper. "This looks interesting."

She ripped it open. But it was only a large tapestry frame. We all stared glumly.

Wally opened the door. "Come on! Come on!"

I followed him with the case. "We're going, Katie."

We waited by the top of the stairs. But Katie didn't follow.

I was just going back for her when we heard a noise.

A key turned in the hall door.

Wally paled in terror. "Shit! A few minutes and we'd have been gone." He put his head in his hands.

"Oh, shut up!" I heard myself say. There was no point in panicking now.

Then everything went into slow motion. The door was pushed open and there was the noise of someone coming in. Then it slammed shut. I looked down to the hall, but couldn't see who it was. There were footsteps on the stairs. We were trapped. What were we to do now?

But Wally sprang into action. "Quick! We'll have to hide! Then get out later!"

We tiptoed back into the bedroom.

"Someone's coming, Katie," I whispered. "We'll have to hide."

She understood immediately. "Can's we get downstairs?"

"It's too risky," I whispered.

"You two get under the bed! I'll hide in the wardrobe!"

In a second Katie was inside the wardrobe. I shut the door then followed Wally under the bed.

We lay there sandwiched together. What would happen if we were caught? We were two normal Irish girls on a working holiday in London. There were probably hundreds or thousands doing the same thing. Yet we'd had nothing but disaster from the start. And now we'd broken into someone's home, like criminals. What would our Grandfather say? "Oh, Angel of God," I prayed, "my guardian dear ... " But it was no use. The words had gone out of my head. Was it Mrs Hanna on the stairs? Christianity was a myth to me, yet I tried to pray again. "Dear God, don't let her come in here!"

The footsteps on the stairs came closer.

And closer.

Wally's eyes were shut tightly.

The door opened.

I was afraid to breathe. Oh, God, was it really happening?

Through the white bedspread, I saw black high heels. They were Mrs Hanna's. I could hear her breathing. Surely she could hear us? She took off something, probably a coat and threw it onto the bed.

Has Anyone Seen Heather?

Then other garments. Then she seemed to be getting out of a corset. Maybe if she went to bed and fell asleep, we could sneak out. Or maybe she'd go to the bathroom across the hall?

But then there was a silence.

Heather's case. In my panic, I'd forgotten to hide it.

The woman pulled up the bedspread and saw us.

"Aghhhhhh!" she screamed.

Everything was up.

I heard Katie jump out of the wardrobe and run.

Then Wally came to life, pushing me out in front of him. "Run, Clare!"

I grabbed the case and we ran past the shocked woman to the stairs. She was in a slip and stood absolutely speechless, clutching her heart. At last she lunged after us. "You again! I'll see you in jail!"

We tore down the stairs two at a time. On the first landing, I dropped the case.

"Leave it!" Wally ordered.

I ran back. We were up creeksville now, but somewhere I'd got courage. Sister Martin was right about grace coming when you needed it. Mrs Hanna was pounding down the stairs after us, but we reached the hall well ahead of her.

Wally struggled with the hall door.

"Won't it open?" I whispered.

He was completely red in the face and pulled feverishly at the lock with his small hands. "It's on some sort of double lock."

I tried, but it was no use.

We were done for.

Then Katie ran into a room. "In here!"

We followed. It was the little room we'd been shown into on our first morning in London. We slammed the door shut just in time. Then, while Wally held it, I jammed a chair under the handle.

"Open the door!" Mrs Hanna pushed and pounded.

Even in my own terror, I marvelled at her persistence. There were three of us and one of her. What if we were dangerous? Why wasn't she afraid of us attacking her? I'd always heard it was better not to confront criminals.

"Open the door!" she screamed.

Thump!

Thump!

Katie heaved the front window open. "We can get out this way."

She stepped deftly through the window onto the sill and jumped over the spiked railings to land in front of the hall door. "Pass me the case!"

I tried, but somehow it dropped to the ground in front of the basement window. I couldn't get back over those railings.

"Leave it!" Wally shouted.

So I jumped down to Katie.

As Wally followed, his running shoe caught in the railings. He struggled to free himself.

I almost died. "Leave it!"

He still struggled.

"Take it off!" I begged.

With one mighty wrench, he freed his foot. Then jumped down to join us. As we tore down Walton Street in the opposite direction to Beauchamp Place, the hall door of the house opened behind us. I turned to see Mrs Hanna running after us in her dressing-gown. Luckily we were faster and made it to the corner.

"Let's get lost in Harrods!" I shouted. "She'll never find us there."

Although people stared, we kept on running through

side streets until we came to Harrods Men's Shop. She could hardly follow us in there. Not in her dressing gown. Inside the shop we walked slowly past a security guard, getting our breath back as we mingled idly with the crowds. I kept glancing nervously behind me. But she hadn't followed us. We went through the food section with its acres of hams into the main part of the shop, going out again on the other side. We had lost her.

Twenty-three

We split up at the Underground. Wally took the bus back to his digs and we went by train to ours. He was ashen-faced and we were both utterly shaken. Even when we got to Bankside, we were still trembling. What had we done? Would we be found out?

There was a man sitting in a car outside our house.

It was too dark to see his face. Could it be Dad? Heather might have sent him. No, he was too thin. Who was it? Nervously I pulled Katie on.

But he called out the window, "Clare Kelly?"

I turned, my heart stopping. Oh, God, were we caught after all? "Yes."

He got out of the car, flashing an ID "Police. Oxford Street Station."

We were definitely up creeksville now. He'd been sent by Mrs Hanna. But how had she found out where we were? Did she have supernatural powers?

Katie was biting her lip.

I gave her a silencing look. I'd do the talking.

The policeman was pleasant-looking, in plain clothes with an anorak instead of a jacket. I can't explain my irrational fear of any policeman. Maybe it had been so traumatic that day in Piccadilly.

"I'd like a little chat with you girls," he said.

I felt myself trembling. "Eh - now?"

He smiled. "If you wouldn't mind. Can I come in?"

"It's a bit late," Katie said.

"Yes!" I added. "We have to be up early."

He rubbed his ear. "It won't take long."

My sister yawned widely. "But we're tired."

I knew she was playing for time. By tomorrow we'd be gone. We'd be somewhere else. Away from this benighted land.

He took out his notebook. "I'm afraid it can't wait!"

A Beresford Clarke later told me that he'd no right to question us. Or to come in without a warrant. But I let him into our room. What else could I do? One thought and one thought alone utterly paralysed me. The dog had barked, because there was a dog. Mrs Hanna had called the police on us because she had nothing to hide. Heather would now be found guilty of theft. And we were being watched all the time. It was too much of a coincidence for him to be waiting for us. He probably knew we'd been to see Heather. Maybe even followed us there. He'd arrest us now. Then her. We'd all end up in jail or reform school.

Katie, of course, hadn't made her bed. Her clothes were strewn everywhere. She's the untidiest person.

I cleared our one chair for the policeman.

He sat down. "Thanks."

We sat on the bed.

Has Anyone Seen Heather?

I expected the usual spiel you saw in films about having the right to remain silent, etc. But he just offered us a cigarette.

Katie, of course, took one.

He lit her up.

I glared at her. She'd lost all shame and become utterly depraved, smoking and drinking. And how would I explain her hair and leopard dress to Grandfather?

He flipped back the cover of a small reporter's notebook. "You girls were employed at the Imperial Hotel at Lancaster Gate until 14th July of this year?"

"Yes." I was relieved. It was something to do with the hotel. Maybe Mrs Hanna hadn't sent him. "We left then."

"On 4th July you both witnessed an alleged rape on Mary Murphy by a certain French man?"

I nodded.

He scanned both our faces. "And you left of your own free will?"

I nodded, looking meaningfully at Katie.

"You're sure?"

"Yes!"

"No one threatened you?"

I played for time. "I don't know what you mean."

"Did anyone threaten you?"

I shook my head. Could he possibly know about the phone calls? Our hate letter? Our suspect chocolates? But if we mentioned them it might come out about Mrs Hanna and our break-in. We might be on some walkie-talkie system. Two Irish girls wanted for breaking and entering.

"Why did you change jobs?" he persisted.

I still couldn't mention Mrs Hanna. If I said she was hounding us, it might come out about the picture being

Has Anyone Seen Heather?

in the pawn shop. He might have been sent by her. All was lost. I imagined the three of us in a dock in front of a wigged judge. Mr Livingstone was rich and powerful. He'd win any fight in court.

"There's no need to be frightened. You've done nothing wrong."

"What?" I mumbled. So he wasn't going to arrest us.

"Why did you change jobs?"

"We had a row with the chef," I said at last.

"And that's the reason you left?"

"He threw eggs at me," Katie said.

"The pay's better here," I added. "We're getting double the money."

Still he went on as if he didn't believe us. "You weren't upset about the sexual assault on your friend?"

Katie coughed over her cigarette. "She wasn't really a friend."

He cleared his throat. "Still, it couldn't have been pleasant."

"It wasn't," I said. What was he getting at?

"Have you been contacted by this Frenchman?"

I shook my head. "He doesn't know where we are."

The policeman, apparently satisfied, snapped his notebook shut. "We're keeping an eye on him. We may need you as witnesses. We're trying to persuade your friend to press charges."

"I tried to."

He stood up. "She wouldn't charge him. But we may still need you. Will you contact us if you change address?"

I was breathing normally now. "Yes."

He walked to the door, looking at us kindly. "There's no need to be so nervous. You've done nothing wrong."

I looked at him innocently.

He laughed. "You'd think you were in Soviet

Has Anyone Seen Heather?

Russia!"

So far it might be better than England's green and pleasant land. But I didn't say so. We were saved again. We'd got into the habit of feeling so guilty about everything. But this time we had cause. Yet he'd come for a perfectly good reason. To check that we were willing and able to testify in the assault against Mary. When we'd almost forgotten the crime. It seemed so long ago. It'd been sordid, but the hotel was another world now. And it was always only second to Heather. So much for human nature. Ask yourself, 'Enry 'Iggins: What do we really care about others, about people not in our own family?

Wally went back to Ireland that week - he had to repeat an exam and needed time to study. So we were alone again. Although we'd escaped, the break-in shattered my nerves. It'd been a crazy idea. We'd achieved absolutely nothing. How had things turned out like this? I was someone who won book prizes in school and got A's in exams. But now I was a common criminal. Heather only had us. But instead of extricating her from the mess she was in, we'd probably got her in deeper. Although we were only trying to help, we'd acted like criminals. Mr Livingstone would hear of it and now be certain she'd stolen the picture. He'd think we were some sort of accomplices, stealing other things, when we were only trying to find the ticket. Maybe he'd sent for the police. They'd find Heather and she might be prosecuted. It'd get into the papers. She'd never be able to get another job. And her future as a companion might be threatened. I told myself she could work at something else, but it still tormented me. What else could she do? She had got married in college and had no qualifications. Now she'd be completely dependent on

Dad. He might hit her again. Everything was my fault. I'd started everything by begging to come over. Why couldn't I believe she was short of money? That she was doing her best? That she couldn't afford us?

Everyday I expected the police to find us. That Mrs Hanna would call them. I was paralysed with fear. And back in the dilemma of not knowing what to do. Wally's last advice was to knock on the door and ask to see Mr Livingstone. "Explain where the painting is. Give him the money to redeem it."

But how could we do that now? After we'd broken into his home. He'd probably have us arrested before we could say anything. I just pictured Grandfather's face, if that happened. He'd say we'd turned out just like Heather and Dad. That we were unreliable and he'd have nothing more to do with us. And who would blame him?

I rang to check on Heather. I was afraid to tell her about our break-in. So I just said we'd been to the pawn shop and she'd have to swear with a solicitor that she'd lost the ticket. That she had only seven days to do this. She promised to ring them and swear the oath in Maidenhead and we weren't to interfere anymore.

"I've written to Mr Livingstone explaining everything, Clare. The picture will be returned as soon as Dad comes back to London," she said.

I certainly didn't want to show up at Walton Street again. Anyhow we were too young to collect the picture. It gets me the way people think you're too young to do things. Adults certainly don't do a very good job of running things. "Was Mr Livingstone mad?" I asked.

"No. He wrote back, saying he trusted me."

Why hadn't she done that in the beginning? Then we

needn't have broken in. Our story was ending, not with a bang, but with a whimper. Again we were sort of suspended in time, waiting for Dad to contact us. Heather said he was travelling in Scotland with a theatre and would be back in London any day now.

I also rang A to say we'd found Heather, but got no answer. The detective business must've picked up because he was never in. There was only a message on an answering machine, saying he'd call back at the earliest opportunity. Finally I left a message thanking him and asking him to send a bill for any fees. I said that we'd found Heather and she was OK and we were going back to Ireland soon. I hoped he wouldn't charge me too much for finding out about the chocolates. We'd never find out why Mrs Hanna was hounding us. Or even if she was. He'd never believed us anyway. And I was even beginning to believe we'd imagined the whole thing. Actually I was relieved A had lost interest - not that he ever had much. I was ashamed to tell him Heather had borrowed the picture. And as for us breaking in. Well, I daren't tell anyone that.

But the very next day A came into the pub - Just as we were clearing up after lunch. Katie was helping me wash the glasses.

I expected him to say I told you so, or see what idiots you girls are. But for a change there was nothing jeering about him. He said in a deadpan voice. "I got your message. Was your Ma all right?"

"Yes, you were right. Her letter went astray." I shrugged nonchalantly, trying to hide my embarrassment. I didn't want him to know about her pawning the picture. Or about our break-in.

He mopped his forehead with a hankie. He has this habit of sweating. "Well, that's a relief. Give me a double Scotch!"

"And she didn't steal any picture," Katie added.

I rolled my eyes at her. Why was she such a blabber? "She only *borrowed* it."

He frowned. "What do you mean borrowed it?"

I poured his drink, explaining about the pawn shop.

He took a swig of whiskey. "Hmm ... I might have guessed. Technically that's theft."

I reddened in anger. "You've always been against her!"

He pointed a finger at me. "Quiet, please!"

I felt tears coming. He had an angry streak which frightened me. And there was something new in his tone. Something serious.

"And don't start that!" He rattled the ice in his glass, staring into it. "There's more to this than your mother thinks."

We looked at each other. "What do you mean?"

"Fasten your seat belt, we're in for a bumpy ride," he said in his American accent. "It turns out you were right. Someone doesn't like you girls." He paused, sort of dramatically, then changed to his gravelly voice. "Because your sweeties were poisoned."

Katie let out a shriek. "I told you!"

I stared at him. "You're sure?"

"Of course, I'm sure! Do you take me for a sap?" Then, turning on my sister, "And there's no need to dance a jig! One of those chocs would've done you in good."

But Katie wasn't to be subdued. "But it proves that Mrs Hanna's a murderess!"

"It proves nothing of the sort!" he growled.

"What were they poisoned with?" I asked warily.

My sister's eyebrows shot up. She was weirdly delighted. "Arsenic?"

He held up his hand in silence. "If you'll be quiet, I'll

Has Anyone Seen Heather?

tell you." Then he pulled a typed sheet of paper out of his pocket and put on a pair of gold rimmed glasses. "I have the report here. They found an odd mixture of things - Atropine, which is Deadly Nightshade. And Spartine, a drug to promote labour in women."

"Labour in women?" I thought I was hearing things. I mean, for God's sake.

Katie giggled nervously.

"It's not funny! Oddly enough there was also an antidote to Spartine - Pilocarpine hydrochloride."

They were all Greek to me. "What'd that do?"

"One would cancel the other," Katie snapped.

"For once she's right." A folded the report. "One would work against the other. It killed your Mr Rat though." He blew out little puffs of air onto his hand.

"So you believe us?" Katie looked self-righteous.

A sipped his drink, frowning. "There's something odd going on."

I was worried. What if our tormentor found out where we were? And tried again?

"At least they want to scare you off." A was looking thoughtfully into his drink.

"Were there any finger prints?" Katie asked suddenly.

He grimaced. "Nothing definite." Then pointed meaningfully at my sister. "Someone had rubbed them all out!"

"But you're meant to handle things with gloves on."

"You can also rub out evidence, Miss Marple!"

She ignored that. "It proves we were right to break in!"

There was a terrible silence. You could almost touch it.

He searched my face. "What do you mean?"

"Oh, we had a look around Mr Livingstone's house,"

I said casually. "Heather needed the pawn ticket. It was with her stuff."

His breath came in little pants like a steam engine. "You mean you broke into the house?"

I nodded, looking guiltily at my sister.

"Did you expect to find a body in the library?" he jeered.

"We only wanted her stuff," I said. "But we dropped it, escaping."

"You were seen?"

I nodded. "Mrs Hanna chased us out."

Luckily people wandered into the Bar then, expecting to be served. So I turned away from A, afraid of his anger. And Katie got her drinks and left. When I was free again, he snapped, "I want a chat with you, Miss!"

"I'm working!" I turned to another customer. "Can I help you?"

"A gin and tonic, love!"

"A pint of shandy and a half of bitter!"

I kept on working, hoping A would leave, but he sat there till closing time. When I went outside with Katie, he was waiting. "I want to talk to you!"

"Both of us?" I asked.

"No. I don't deal with children!"

He ordered Katie back to the house, then walked me back and forth outside the pub, ranting and raving. I'd never seen anyone so angry - not even Dad. He was furious. With me? Me? When I'd tried to stop them. It was all Katie's idea. She was standing in the doorway of our digs and hearing everything. I was always picking up the tab for her. It was the story of my life. In school, everywhere. From the year dot. Although I pretended I didn't care, I was mortified to be told off like some little kid. Especially in front of Katie. I hated him. And he really frightened me. He kept saying, "You realise you could be in serious trouble?"

I nodded.

"He might press charges. As you're eighteen you could go to prison. And your sister to reform school."

My fear nearly choked me. But he just went on and on, telling me I was a bad example to my sister. That he was sorry he'd ever had anything to do with us. It had been the biggest mistake of his life. Why had I nagged my mother? That he didn't blame our father for disappearing. That really got me. I started crying, of course. He went into his Bogart imitation about not pulling that stunt on him so I stopped.

He turned on me furiously. "Do you still want my help?"

I nodded.

"All right!" He wagged a finger threateningly. "Will you do what I say?"

"Y-yes," I said.

But he was looking over at Katie. "What about Miss Marple?"

She came over. "I will!"

"No more taking the law into your own hands."

We agreed and he seemed placated.

"Now I want you to think back. Did you make any enemies in London?"

We looked at each other, puzzled.

"You didn't meet anyone on the boat over?"

I shook my head no.

"Anyone in the hotel?"

"It wasn't very nice there," Katie said. "Someone tried to rape another girl."

"What?" A looked up, shocked.

I sighed wearily. "We walked in on him."

Then it all came out about the French professor.

Has Anyone Seen Heather?

He pulled me up. "That could be important. Why didn't you tell me?"

I shrugged. He'd never have believed us, but I couldn't remind him of that. It'd be like saying I told you so or something. Finally, he left, having confirmed details about where Heather had left the picture, the date and how much she had pawned it for. He took our wad of money, saying he had ways of making them release it. Despite his shouting, A was now utterly committed to us. He didn't even mention money for his fee. We must owe him a good bit. I think the chocolates had really shocked him. We were back in the twilight world of poison and paranoia. The news put Katie on a sort of high. But I was back in my nightmare.

I longed to be back in Dublin with Heather. For a normal life of school and even hockey which I could never before stand. A phrase kept running through my head: "*In the Indian summer of my days ...*" I couldn't remember the rest. Maybe Heather and Grandfather could have an Indian summer in their relationship. Maybe it wasn't too late. I just wanted Heather to get better so we could take her home to Grandfather. At least temporarily. I was fed up with London.

I rang Heather that evening.

"I'm being discharged in about two weeks, darling," she said. "Dad's collecting me. Then we're going to live in London."

I didn't want her to count on him. "But what about our flat?"

"Clare, darling. You still have school. I want you to go back to Grandad."

I caught my breath. "Won't you come with us?"

"We'll have to wait and see. For the moment, you're to go home."

What did she mean 'home'? How could it be home without her? But she sounded firm for the first time in her life. So much for our plans.

I didn't upset her by mentioning the chocolates. I just told her a friend was retrieving the painting and bringing it back to Mr Livingstone. That he'd be ringing her about swearing the oath with the solicitor.

Twenty-four

The next morning A phoned me, saying I was to get the afternoon off. Mr Williams kindly agreed to both of us going if we made it up on our next day off. He was good about that. So immediately after lunch, A came into the pub, carrying a brown leather briefcase.

"Get your coat," he snapped at me.

I asked where were we going.

He patted the brief case. "I have the painting here. I've made an appointment with Mr Livingstone. We're going to return it. And sort out some other little matters. You're going to apologise for one thing!"

My stomach churned with nerves. "Can Katie come too?"

He shook his head grimly. "Just you!"

"But he might call the police," I said.

He nodded. "Yes. That's likely. Now hurry up!"

"But I can't leave her. If I'm arrested, she won't manage without me."

He ground his teeth. "You promised to *do as you are told*!"

I stood firm. I said we did everything together. And even if we had to go to prison, we'd go together. In the end he gave in, driving us across London in an old battered Honda. It seemed centuries since our first London taxi ride the morning of our arrival. Yet it was only six and a half weeks. Time is an illusion. Wally was right. For so long it had stood agonisingly still, and now it was hurtling downhill like a car without breaks.

On the steps of Mr Livingstone's I wanted to throw up. If only we didn't have to face him. It was like being brought to the Reverend Mother in school. We'd acted stupidly, but at least we hadn't tried to kill anyone like Mrs Hanna. Katie was pale too. Her hair was getting a bit longer now and blew in light feathers around her face. She looked so young in her leopard mini. And pudgy from all the pizzas.

Luckily another woman showed us in. "Are you Mr Beresford Clarke?"

And when A nodded, she said politely, "Mr Livingstone is expecting you. Just wait in here."

And we were shown into the little room from which we had escaped and in which we had first met Mr Livingstone. So much had happened since that first morning in London. We were different people now.

I breathed deeply to control my nerves. A plonked down on a chintzy couch, signalling us to do the same.

He took out the famous painting and laid it carefully across his knee. It was murky OK, but really delicate and beautiful. A watercolour woodscene in deep browns. "He'll be glad enough to have this back."

Katie admired it over his shoulder.

Then the door opened. Mr Livingstone was wheeled

in by Mrs Hanna. She looked as if she'd like to kill us. I wanted to faint. How could he stand to be near her?

A stood up. "Mr Livingstone, sir. We have your property."

The sick man smiled faintly. He looked very weak. But he smiled kindly at us. "I'm glad you knocked this time."

"I'm sorry ..." I looked away in embarrassment.

Katie fidgeted awkwardly. "Me too."

He looked grave, speaking with some effort. "You gave poor Mrs Hanna a bad fright."

"We didn't mean to," I mumbled.

A nodded approvingly.

Mr Livingstone seemed appeased. Although Mrs Hanna just glared through her thick glasses. I know people can't help their looks, but she looked like a bully. Heavy-set and muscley.

A held up the painting. "You can see, it's perfectly all right, not damaged in any way. Mrs Kelly brought it to be valued as she told you. Then pawned it on the way home. But got ill before she could redeem it. It was stupid, but not quite criminal."

Mr Livingstone perused the painting. "It seems to have been a misunderstanding."

"She was bringing it back," I mumbled.

"I know, my dear. We were all a bit hasty."

Mrs Hanna bristled aggressively. "You're not letting them off scot free! They're downright vandals."

At that A cleared his throat, taking the poisoned chocolates out of his bag. He slammed them down on the table beside the painting. "Do you recognise this, Mrs Hanna?"

She looked at the box curiously. "I've never seen them before in my life."

I searched her face. I have to admit she didn't

register shock or anything at being found out. She just looked curious. Genuinely curious. It wasn't the look of a murderess. Maybe we'd been wrong about her.

Then A handed her our anonymous note. "Do you know anything about this?"

She blinked behind her glasses as she read it. "I don't know what you're implying. Those girls are liars! They've invented this. And they had an accomplice! A young man!"

Mr Livingstone coughed gently. "Don't be harsh, Mrs Hanna. They're only wains." Then he read the note, looking at us. "This melodrama must've been stirred up by someone else, my dears. Neither I nor Mrs Hanna know anything about it."

A put the box back in his briefcase. "Good! I'll bring them to the police. First I had to be sure no one here was involved."

And so we left, this time carrying our mother's case. And by the hall door and not the window. I wanted to go back to Ireland as soon as possible. I still hoped to persuade Heather to come. But I couldn't walk out on Mr Williams. William Shakespeare's had been like a family to us. If we left without notice, Liz would only have to do our job. So we went back and gave a proper week's notice. Our days of flitting were over. A rang the next day. "Well, I've found your poisoner."

"Oh," I said shakily. It still seemed shocking and utterly unbelievable that someone wanted us out of the way. Murdered.

"Why didn't you tell me about that Frenchman sooner?" he said.

"It didn't seem important. Anyhow you wouldn't have believed us."

He laughed shortly. "You're probably right there. Well, he's your phantom poisoner, anonymous caller and weird note sender. All in one."

It was hard to believe. "Are you sure?"

"Yes. He sent another box. To a member of the police force. A woman ate one. You were lucky girls. They told me they sent someone from Special Branch to question you."

Then I remembered the policeman waiting for us the night we came back from finding Heather. "Yes ... they did."

"Why didn't you tell me?"

"I thought he was just checking - that we were willing to give evidence."

"You should've told me."

I felt myself redden. Was he going to have another fit? "Is the woman OK?" I asked, changing the subject.

"She's in hospital. Seriously ill."

I was shocked. God, only for Katie we could have been badly hurt. She was the one who suspected they were poisoned. "But we didn't do anything to him!"

A sighed. "He knew that Mary might be persuaded to press charges. He thought you'd testify against him. You were the only people who saw the assault. He was watching you. When you didn't respond to his note or phone calls, he decided to put you into hospital."

It was unbelievable. "Where is he now?"

"Locked up. He was crazy, Clare. He tried to rape a woman in another hotel. They got him, though. The police will be in touch with you. You may still have to give evidence in court."

"But we'll be back at school."

He cleared his throat. "So you're going home? I'm glad about that. Well, keep looking up!"

And before I could ask about his fee, he hung up.

I was sad not to be seeing him again. He'd been nice to us in his own queer way. Funny how it all turned out to be true. We were being hounded, but by someone we never suspected. Sometimes the solution is so obvious. It's under your nose all the time and you can't see it.

Heather was amazed too. We visited her again in the hospital. She let us come down on the condition that we'd go back to Grandfather. So I rang Brigid, saying we'd be home at the end of the week. She said I'd done OK in my exams, but Grandfather had a bone to pick with me about Irish. To prepare myself for a lecture. Irish? Things like that were another life. And utterly inconsequential after our summer. Of course, I didn't say anything about bringing Heather home. To the end, I still hoped to persuade her. What could Grandfather say if we just arrived back with her? Could he turn out his own child? Blood is meant to be thicker than water.

But it was a truth I had to discover for myself.

As I was walking across the bar about two days later, someone called gently, "Clare."

I looked up. The accent was American.

It was Dad.

I stared, speechless. I hadn't seen him for nearly four years. But there he was, still tall and handsome. With his skimpy brown hair. But thinner. Much thinner. Both in hair and body.

"Don't you know your old man?" he said shyly. He has Katie's awkward shyness.

I ran to him. I couldn't help it. "Daddy!"

He kissed me in front of everyone, swinging me up, like when I was little. "You look lovely, my dear. And you've grown!"

"You're looking well too," I mumbled, pulling back and remembering to be angry.

He patted the front of his jacket. He always looked

sort of rumpled. But his white shirt was clean and he had a nice yellow jumper. "I've lost a bit. I'm off the sauce, Clare. I've joined AA."

I said nothing.

"Can I have another chance?"

"You hit Heather," I said. I just couldn't help it.

His blue eyes looked so sad, I started crying. I don't know why, when I'd resented him so much, for so long. But you have to forgive people.

"Come on, Clare." He touched my shoulder awkwardly.

"Everything's been awful! We didn't know where Heather was."

"Now, Clare. It's - Heather's told me everything."

I wiped my eyes. "We've been so worried ..."

"I know." He put his arm round me.

"You could've written."

He sighed deeply. "Clare, I'm a bastard. But I was afraid."

I pulled away. "Afraid of what?"

"Of you."

"Of me?"

"I was afraid you wouldn't answer."

I just looked at him. How could he think I wouldn't answer?

We couldn't thank him for the kilts, because we had no address.

"Where's Katie?" he said, breaking the silence.

"She's working in the restaurant."

"Be my ally, Clare." His eyes pleaded.

Katie wasn't off till three. Although I offered to get her, he wanted to wait. So he sat in the bar, nervously drinking coke. I couldn't believe it. *Coke?* It used to be vodka and coke in a *pint* glass, all day long. AA must work. In between customers, I went over and he chatted about the future. He was going back to Heather. I tried to imagine them together. What would it be like to have a father again? Would we be a normal family? And have Sunday lunch together like the rest of the universe?

At closing time, Katie collected me as usual. When she saw Dad, she froze.

He stared. I knew he was startled by her beauty. Then he went over and put his arms around her. "Katie."

She smiled like some shy kid.

"Come on, a kiss for your old man."

Of course, they made up. He was our father.

Afterwards he brought us to his bedsit in North London. The area was unbelievably grotty. He lived right at the top of a tall shabby house. On the way up endless flights of steps, we passed Indians coming down. There was a strong smell of curry. And the door to his room had three locks.

"You have to be careful here." He struggled to open it, laughing his low laugh. "The man opposite steals."

But inside was another world. He'd painted the walls white and a mattress was covered with a lovely Indian bedspread. There were nice cups on a clean pine table. And the light was covered with one of those Chinese shades. There were rows of books: novels, works on the theatre, plays and lives of actors. And the small cooker was surrounded with interesting pots and pans.

"I thought you had a bed-sit in Maidenhead," Katie said.

"That was in the beginning. I got some work in a small theatre down there. Now, I'm trying out for a part at the National. It's my big break, girls."

My Dad has big dreams. But at least now he'd stopped drifting. He cooked us a meal that evening -

stir-fried chicken. He'd learnt to cook really well because he'd worked in a restaurant. He'd had all sorts of jobs in the three and three quarter years. But he told us things were picking up in the theatre. He was getting parts. It was what he always said, as far back as I could remember. But maybe this time it was true. Then he said he was bringing Heather back to the flat. They were making a new start in London. They would eventually send for us.

"Can't we come now?" Katie asked.

I was surprised at the change in her. She'd taken him straight to her heart.

Dad shook his head. "There's not enough room, sweetheart. We'll send for you."

I looked away. It was always the same. Maybe this time he'd send a postcard.

"Will you trust me, Clare?"

I nodded, controlling tears. What else could I do?

Maturity's forgiving your parents, Sister Martin told me. You have to forgive them. Even for not wanting you. Which was the case with ours really. Of course, we had to go back to Grandfather - there was nowhere else. It was good to see him and Brigid and the dogs again. We couldn't tell them what happened. How we had travelled so far to find Heather, met witches, and broken into a giant's castle to find lost treasure. Of course, we didn't rescue the Queen or wake her up from her spell. And we're not living happily ever after. I suppose the flat's never to be now. But I miss you, Heather Kelly. And in life anything can happen. You go looking for one parent and find both.

It's now December and they're still together. Of course, Grandfather was a prophet of doom. But for once he's turning out to be wrong. At least, so far. Maybe my pledge is working. We're going to London for a family Christmas. It'll be great, seeing our old haunts again. Mary might still be at the hotel. And we'll definitely call down to Liz at William Shakespeare's. Maybe we'll have a coke with her and Jerry. Maybe one day our parents'll send for us permanently. Or come back home. You have to think cosmically. Things take time. The universe is expanding. And after all, we're only hearing the noise from the Big Bang now. And comets have returned faithfully since the beginning of time. My mistake was agreeing to Heather's going in the first place. I should have known she'd fall under our father's spell. But you can't get upset. You must keep perspective. Our life is the dance of a butterfly. And it's really how you see things. Not what you have.

We're back at school now. But there can be no more dreaming like last year. Things are for real. I've started the Leaving Certificate slog, but still see Wally on Saturday nights. Although we'll always just be friends. I'm more mature now and don't feel the need to flaunt him. Sometimes Katie comes with us. She's doing her Inter. In the meantime she wanted to write down our adventures. So we do it every night. I still have to pinch myself. I mean, it was all so hairy. We were two Patricias, thinking Heather was missing when it was only a case of a letter going astray. Then the professor and the poison chocolates. And all the oddities we met. Jennifer and A, Liz and Jerry. Even the rat was weird. We didn't bother telling anyone in school - they'd never believe us anyhow. My class only thinks about mundane things like mid-term exams. That and hockey's the limit of their experience. Their mothers always picked them up from school. They'd never believe ours could be lost. Or that a professor could be so wicked. So I didn't show them the cutting A

Has Anyone Seen Heather?

Beresford Clarke sent me from the *London Evening Standard*:

SENDING POISON CHOCOLATES BRINGS 15-YEAR SENTENCE

A prominent French Humanities Professor was sentenced yesterday to 15 years in prison for sending posion chocolates to a London police officer. Jean Cartier, who is from Lyons, was also charged with attempting to rape Helga Frankfurter, an employee of the Elizabeth Hotel, Eccelston Square.

"You have sunk to the lowest level of humanity," Judge James Brooke said in court. "The act of rape is terrible enough, and when you follow it up with attempted murder of a police officer, I have no choice but to sentence you severely."

A signed his name *Alan*. "Keep looking up, Clare," he scrawled. "Regards to Miss Marple."

I'm glad they got that creepy Frenchman. We didn't have to be witnesses because Mary never charged him. So it wasn't necessary to send us chocolates. Imagine, if we'd ended up in hospital? I kept the clipping, just to remind myself the summer wasn't a dream. That anything can happen. Maybe it was all to do with tempting fate. If you don't believe me, just you wait, 'Enry 'Iggins. Katie's imagination's definitely over active. I mean, she wanted to start this with something "atmospheric."

Although she's taller than me now, she looks so young in her nightie and bedsocks. She's lost all that puppy fat from the pizzas and her hair's growing out, to Grandfather's great relief - he nearly died when he saw it. So did Brigid. But Katie'll always be beautiful. I'm not jealous. You couldn't be jealous of someone as generous as her. But we still fight sometimes.

"OK," I said "think of something atmospheric."
"It was a stormy night ..."
I said nothing. After all, the whole summer had been a string of clichés. But when things began it was a morning, pale and calm. And we were two girls having breakfast in our grandfather's kitchen. Everything was dead ordinary. But my sister wants to be a sleuth, and thinks she's Agatha Christie.

BRIGHT SPARKS

DAISY CHAIN WAR

Joan O'Neill

Set in Dublin during the late thirties and forties, this is the story of cousins, Irish Lizzie and English Vicky, growing up during 'The Emergency'. All the hopes and yearnings, the fears and achievements of teenage life are captured in this enchanting novel of everyday life in wartime Ireland.

£4.99